THE
ILIAD

First published 2015 by Walker Books Ltd
87 Vauxhall Walk, London SE11 5HJ

This edition published 2018

2 4 6 8 10 9 7 5 3 1

Text © 2015 Gillian Cross
Illustrations © 2015 Neil Packer

The right of Gillian Cross and Neil Packer to be identified as author and illustrator respectively
of this work has been asserted by them in accordance with the Copyright, Designs and Patents Act 1988

This book has been typeset in Skia

Printed and bound in China

British Library Cataloguing in Publication Data:
a catalogue record for this book is available from the British Library

ISBN 978-1-4063-8561-8

www.walker.co.uk

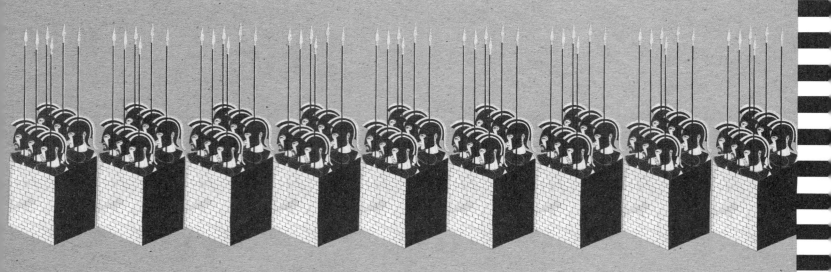

THE ILIAD

RETOLD BY Gillian Cross

ILLUSTRATED BY Neil Packer

WALKER BOOKS
AND SUBSIDIARIES
LONDON · BOSTON · SYDNEY · AUCKLAND

CONTENTS

This is the story of a bitter quarrel between two proud and powerful men. It brought death to hundreds of brave heroes and destroyed one of the great cities of the world. And yet it started with something very small...

THE GOLDEN APPLE

IT ALL BEGAN WITH AN APPLE. A golden apple, engraved with dangerous words.

FOR THE MOST BEAUTIFUL.

Three goddesses tried to claim it. But which of them really was the most beautiful? Was it Hera, wife of Zeus, king of the gods? Or Athene, the goddess of wisdom? Or Aphrodite, the goddess of love?

To settle the argument, they left their home on high Olympus and went to find Paris, Prince of Troy, the most handsome man in the world. As he stood alone on Mount Ida, they appeared in front of him, in all their loveliness.

"Who should have this apple?" they said. "Choose one of us!"

Paris was dazzled and terrified. But the three goddesses were determined to have an answer. They began to offer him bribes.

"Choose me!" said Hera. "I will give you power and make you a great ruler."

"Choose me!" said Athene. "You will win all your battles and become a famous warrior."

Aphrodite smiled silkily. "Choose me," she murmured, "and you shall have the most beautiful woman in the world for your wife."

Aphrodite's bribe was the one that delighted Paris. But it cast a long and deadly shadow. The most beautiful woman in the world was Helen of Sparta – and she was already married, to Sparta's king, Menelaus. Aphrodite knew that, but she promised Helen to Paris – and he stretched out his hand and gave her the apple.

And the quarrel that began on Olympus boiled over into the human world.

Paris set out to steal the King of Sparta's wife, with Aphrodite's help. He was already handsome, but she made him irresistible. Dazzled and entranced, Helen left her husband and she and Paris ran off to Troy together – with a ship full of Spartan treasure.

Menelaus was outraged. So was his brother Agamemnon, High King over all the Greeks. The two brothers called on the other kings of Greece to help them fetch Helen back.

The quarrel that started with an apple spread wider and wider. In every part of Greece, kings gathered their armies. Fleets of long ships set sail for Troy, carrying heroes with names that will live for ever: quick-witted Odysseus of Ithaca; wise old Nestor, king of Pylos; valiant Diomedes from Argos and noble Ajax, who ruled Salamis.

Mightiest of all was Achilles, the great runner, son of the sea-nymph Thetis. His bronze armour gleamed as he led his fierce Myrmidon soldiers on board their ships.

The Greeks attacked as soon as they landed on the Trojan coast. But Troy was not an easy city to conquer. It was protected by rivers on two sides, and surrounded by strong, high walls. And King Priam, Paris's father, refused to hand Helen back. Instead, he called on his allies to help him defend the city.

He had fifty sons too, every one of them ready to fight for Helen and her treasure. They were all brave men, but the bravest of all, and the noblest warrior, was Prince Hector, tamer of horses.

The Greeks could not fight their way into Troy, but they refused to leave without Helen. Pulling their long ships up on the beach, they built huts on the shore and settled down to lay siege to the city.

No one guessed how long it would take. Nine years later, they were still there, living in the same cramped huts. They were still fighting battles on the plain in front of Troy, still trying to breach the city walls.

They would not give up and abandon the war, but all of them longed for the homes they had left behind in Greece.

No wonder they began to quarrel among themselves...

APHRODITE

APOLLO

PRIAM

HECTOR

PARIS

HECUBA

HELEN

AENEAS

DOLON

BRISEIS

ATHENE   HERA

AGAMEMNON   ACHILLES   ODYSSEUS

AJAX   PATROCLUS   MENELAUS

DIOMEDES   NESTOR

THE QUARREL

||||||||||||||||||||||||||||||||||||||||||||||||||||||||

LIKE THE QUARREL that started the war in the first place, this new quarrel was about a woman. The Greeks had captured several Trojans and Agamemnon had seized a beautiful girl called Chryseis. Her father was a priest of the god Apollo and he wanted his daughter back. He came to the Greek ships with a cart full of treasure, determined to ransom her.

But Agamemnon refused to take the treasure. He treated the old man rudely, and sent him away.

Apollo was furious at the insult to his priest. He swooped down on the Greek ships with arrows carrying plague. Day and night, for nine days, he shot the arrows at mules, dogs and men. The whole Greek camp was devastated by disease and death.

Achilles realized why the plague had hit them.

"It's your fault," he said to Agamemnon. "Let the old priest take his daughter back. Otherwise we'll have to give up and go home."

Agamemnon flew into a rage. "You've taken captives too. Why should I give up mine while you hang on to yours? If I have to send Chryseis back, I want another woman instead. You can give me one of yours. I'll take Briseis!"

15

"Why should I suffer?" Achilles shouted. "My men and I deserve some reward for fighting your war. If you're going to take everything away, we might as well go home. *We* have no quarrel with the Trojans!"

"I am your King!" thundered Agamemnon. "You have sworn to obey my orders!"

That was true, but Achilles refused to back down. Storming off to his hut, he ordered all his men to withdraw from the fighting.

Agamemnon knew there was only one way to end the plague. He had to give up the old priest's daughter. But he was in command of the Greek army, and he couldn't allow Achilles to defy him. So when he sent Chryseis back to her father, he dispatched two of his soldiers to Achilles' hut, to fetch Briseis.

Briseis didn't want to go with them. When she came out of the hut, she was crying bitterly. But Agamemnon's orders had to be obeyed. The soldiers hustled her away and Achilles was left alone, staring out to sea.

He wept with rage and humiliation. "How can Zeus treat me like this?" he shouted across the water. "Doesn't he care about me?"

Deep in the ocean, his mother Thetis heard him. She came floating up through the clear blue water and drifted on to the beach.

"Why so sad?" she said, stroking her son with a hand delicate as mist.

Achilles told her, bitterly. He was furious and he wanted revenge –

whatever it cost other people. "I want to see the Greek army on the run," he said. "Go and plead with Zeus to help the Trojans. When the Greek army is penned in among these ships – when his soldiers are being slaughtered – maybe Agamemnon will realize how stupid he was to lose me and my Myrmidons!"

Thetis gazed at him with her eyes full of tears.

She knew he was fated to die young. How could she refuse him anything when he had such a short time to live? "I'll go straight to Zeus," she said. Leaving Achilles on the shore, she flew to Mount Olympus, where the gods watch over the human world. She flung herself at Zeus's feet and clasped his knees.

"Mighty Father," she said, "you know that my dear son Achilles is doomed to die young. Now Agamemnon has robbed and insulted him. Give Achilles his revenge! Let the Trojans win every battle until justice is done."

Zeus looked down at her and sighed. The gods were divided over the war in Troy and Hera, his wife, was a fierce supporter of the Greeks. But Thetis was looking up at him with tears in her lovely eyes and he couldn't resist her grief. Reluctantly, he nodded.

"I will do it," he said.

First, Zeus sent Agamemnon a false dream, to deceive him. In the dream, Agamemnon saw himself talking to old Nestor, wisest of the Greek kings.

"Get up, Agamemnon!" said the dream-Nestor. "Now is the time to lead your armies out! If you attack now, you will defeat the Trojans and break down the walls of Troy. *Remember this!*"

Agamemnon woke and sat up, shaken by his vivid dream. Calling the other kings together, he told them to prepare for battle.

"I have had a message from Zeus," he said. "We shall win this fight!"

All along the seashore, men began polishing their armour and harnessing the chariot horses. Bronze glittered in the sunlight and the earth shook with the thunder of heroes' feet as the Greeks prepared to attack.

But everything was quiet and still around Achilles' ships. Achilles was sulking inside his hut, refusing to forget his quarrel with Agamemnon. And the Myrmidons were strolling around idly, watching their horses graze. None of them would be part of this battle.

From inside the city, the Trojans saw what the Greeks were doing. At once, they prepared to meet them. They marched out through the Scaean gate and formed lines on a mound called Thorn Hill. But they weren't looking forward to the fight.

And there was still a chance of avoiding a full scale battle.

As the Greek army approached, Paris stepped out

of the Trojan lines. He was dressed in a panther skin, with his bow in his hand.

"Is any Greek brave enough to meet me in single combat?" he shouted. "If we settle the war like that, hundreds of lives will be saved."

Menelaus leapt forward instantly, hungry for the fight. He was eager to kill Paris and win back his wife. Glaring furiously at the Trojans, he began to buckle on his armour.

Inside Troy, King Priam and his councillors were sitting on the city wall, high above the Scaean gate. They didn't hear what Paris said, but they saw what was happening and they leaned together, muttering anxiously.

As they were talking, Helen came walking along

23

the ramparts. She was weeping at the sight of the two armies drawn up for battle and her tears made her lovelier than ever.

"How beautiful she is!" the old men whispered to each other. "But oh – if only she had never come to Troy."

King Priam beckoned her over. "Tell me," he said, "which of these Greek heroes is Agamemnon? Where are Menelaus and Odysseus, Ajax and Diomedes? And which is Achilles?"

Helen looked down from the wall. "Achilles isn't there," she said. "But the tall, handsome man is Agamemnon. And the others—"

One by one, she pointed them out to Priam. The sound of their names made her ache with longing for her lost home in Sparta. But it was too late to undo what had happened. However sad she was, she could not end the war.

Down below, Paris and Menelaus were facing each other, with their weapons in their hands. But, watching over the scene, the goddess Aphrodite had no intention of letting them fight. She knew Menelaus was faster and stronger, and she didn't want to see Paris killed. As Menelaus attacked, she stood beside Paris, ready to protect him.

Menelaus grabbed at Paris's helmet, dragging him off his feet and throttling him with the helmet strap. Quickly, Aphrodite broke the strap and sent Menelaus staggering backwards. Then she wrapped Paris in a thick mist and snatched him away from the battlefield. She whisked him into the city and laid him down on his own soft, scented bed.

24

Menelaus was still trying to fight. But when he threw his spear into the mist it clattered to the ground without hitting anything. Then the mist cleared, and Paris had vanished. Menelaus knew that one of the gods had interfered.

Now there was no chance to stop the battle. The Greek chariots surged forward, like a great wave of the sea, and the two armies clashed head on. With spears and swords and arrows, the killing began.

INSIDE THE WALLS OF TROY

THE GREEKS WERE BITTERLY AWARE that Achilles was missing, but they fought like lions. Diomedes fell on the Trojans like a whirlwind and the goddess Athene went with him, turning the enemy spears away from his chariot. It looked as though the Trojans would be forced back inside the city.

But Hector wasn't ready to be defeated. He leapt down from his chariot and ran along the Trojan lines, shouting encouragement.

"Be brave, my friends! Hold on to your positions! I'll go into the city and offer a sacrifice to the gods. We will not be beaten!"

The Trojans were inspired by his speech. They began to fight even more ferociously. Leaving his cousin Aeneas in charge of the army, Hector strode through the gate and into the city.

27

As he entered his father's palace, he met his mother, Queen Hecuba. She caught hold of his hand, amazed to see him there in the middle of a battle.

"What's happening?" she cried. "Have the Greeks reached our city walls? You must be exhausted. Let me fetch you a cup of wine."

"This is no time for drinking!" Hector said. "We must win Athene over to our side. Take your most beautiful, precious robe to her temple and offer it on the altar. Promise her a splendid sacrifice if she will only save our city. Quickly!"

Hecuba hurried off to do as he asked and Hector went to look for his brother Paris. *He caused all this bloodshed,* he thought angrily. *How dare he skulk inside the city, like a coward?*

He burst into the splendid palace that Paris had built for himself and marched through one room after another, ignoring the servants. Finally, he found Paris in the bedroom, polishing his beautiful armour. Helen sat beside him, doing embroidery.

"Why are you hiding here?" Hector shouted furiously. "All the other Trojan warriors are risking death to keep the Greeks out of Troy. You should be ashamed!"

"I know," said Paris smoothly. "But I was mortified at being snatched away from my fight with Menelaus. I felt so bad that I wanted to hide away, but Helen keeps telling me I should go back to the battle. I'll come with you, if you wait while I strap on my armour."

Helen joined in hastily, trying to calm Hector's anger. "Forgive us both. We know this whole war is our fault. Sit down for a moment while Paris gets ready."

"You're very kind," Hector said coldly, "but I haven't got time to

sit and chatter. I'm going home to see my wife and my son – in case I don't survive this battle."

He hurried away, leaving Paris and Helen in the bedroom. But when he reached his own house Andromache, his wife, wasn't there.

"She heard the battle was going badly," said one of her ladies. "So she ran out to see what was happening. And the nurse went after her, carrying baby Astyanax."

Hector rushed off to find Andromache. As he reached the Scaean gate, she came running towards him with the nursemaid behind her, carrying Astyanax, Hector's darling son.

Andromache burst into tears and caught hold of her husband's hand. "What will I do if you're killed?" she cried. "You're all I have!

Don't make me a widow and leave our son an orphan! Stay inside the city and rally your troops from the top of the Great Tower."

"I can't hide in here like a coward," Hector said gently. "I must do everything I can to keep the Greeks out of Troy. If they win, they'll sack the city and carry you off as slaves. May the earth lie deep over my dead body before that happens!"

He reached out to take his son. But Astyanax had never seen his father in full armour and Hector's huge helmet terrified him. He cowered away from its quivering horsehair plume.

Hector and Andromache laughed tenderly. Hector lifted off his helmet and put it on the ground. Then he took Astyanax in his arms and gave him a kiss.

"May Zeus make you strong and brave," he whispered, "so that men say, 'He's a better man than his father.' May you triumph in battle, and make your mother happy."

He handed the baby to Andromache and she smiled at him through her tears. Deeply moved, Hector stroked her face.

"Try not to grieve," he said. "We can't escape the fate that is fixed for us. Go home and keep our household running smoothly. That's your work, and you do it well. My work is to fight for our city. I must go back to the battle." He put on his helmet and strapped it up.

Andromache started home, with Astyanax in her arms. But she kept looking back at Hector over her shoulder, weeping bitterly. She had a terrible feeling that she would never see him alive again.

As Hector turned towards the gate, Paris came hurrying down to join him, full of life and vigour. His armour gleamed in the sun and he was laughing.

"I'm sorry I kept you waiting," he said. "I know you are eager to get back to the fight."

"I was only trying to protect your reputation," Hector said gravely. "You were the one who plunged us all into this war and I don't want to hear other Trojans calling you a coward. If I'm doing you an injustice, I'll make amends when the war is over – if Zeus lets us win." Without waiting for a reply, he turned away and walked out through the gate.

Back into the battle.

SINGLE COMBAT

||||||||||||||||||||||||||||||||||||||||||||||||||||||

THE SIGHT OF HECTOR AND PARIS revived their troops like a blast of fresh air. The two princes jumped into their chariots.

"Drive straight at the Greek lines!" they ordered their charioteers. As the chariots galloped forward, they both launched their weapons, throwing straight and hard. Two Greeks fell dead on the ground in front of them.

Suddenly the exhausted Trojans were full of energy. Charging forward, they sent their spears hurtling through the air. Now it was the Greeks who were on the defensive. They were forced to give ground.

Athene was horrified to see them falling. She swept down from Mount Olympus but, before she could do anything to help, her way was barred by Apollo.

She glared at him. "I know you support the Trojans."

"And I know you want the Greeks to win," said Apollo. "You

can't wait to see them conquer Troy and burn it to the ground. But wouldn't you like this terrible killing to stop? Just for a while."

Athene looked doubtful. "Is that possible?"

"If we work together," said Apollo, "we can inspire Hector to make a noble gesture. Let's get him to challenge a Greek champion to single combat."

Athene agreed. She and Apollo laid aside their quarrel – for the time being – and went to find Prince Helenus, one of Hector's brothers. He had the gift of second sight and could hear messages from the gods.

They whispered to him and, even in the middle of the fighting, he knew what they were saying. Immediately, he struggled through the battle to Hector's chariot.

"Brother," he said, "I have a message from the gods. Tell the soldiers to stop fighting. Then offer to meet one of the Greeks in single combat. The gods have promised that you won't die."

Hector was delighted by the idea. Stepping into the space between the two armies, he held his spear in front of the Trojans, signalling to them to sit down.

Puzzled and cautious, Agamemnon stepped out to join him, waving his spear so that the Greeks sat down too. With a clatter, the two great armies sank to the ground, facing each other across no-man's-land. Suddenly the whole plain was still and silent.

Athene and Apollo looked down at the great sea of warriors.

Ἀπόλλων

Ἀθήνη

Ὀ. Ἀ. Ἀυ. Μɛ. Δ.

Νɛ.

"Is any Greek brave enough
to face me single-handed?
If so I challenge him
to step forward and
fight me now, in front
of both our armies."

Transforming themselves into vultures, they flew down into a tall oak tree and settled there, waiting to see what would happen.

Hector turned towards the Greek army. "I am Hector, prince of Troy," he shouted. "Is any Greek brave enough to face me single-handed? If so, I challenge him to step forward and fight me now, in front of both our armies. If he kills me, he can take my armour, but he must send my body home to Troy, for a proper funeral. If I kill him, his armour will go to Troy, to hang in Apollo's temple. But I will return his body to your ships, so that you can build him a funeral pyre and make a burial mound for his bones. Who will accept my challenge?"

The Greeks knew what a great warrior he was. They stared at him nervously and no one spoke.

At last, Menelaus scrambled to his feet. "This is shameful!" he yelled at his comrades. "Sit there and rot if you like! I'm going to fight Hector!"

A dozen other Greeks leapt forward to stop him. Everyone knew that Menelaus was no match for Hector.

"Don't throw your life away for nothing, brother," said Agamemnon. "Sit down. We'll find someone to make Hector regret this challenge."

"I'd go if I were young enough!" shouted Nestor. "But I am an old man now – and all the rest of you are cowards!"

His angry accusation had men leaping to their feet. Agamemnon himself was first, followed by great Diomedes of Argos, then Ajax of Salamis and Odysseus of Ithaca – all clamouring to be chosen.

"We'll draw lots," Nestor said wisely. Taking off his helmet, he held it out and each of them marked a stone and dropped it in.

The soldiers knew who were the greatest warriors. As Nestor shook the helmet, the whole Greek army was praying. "Let it be Ajax or Diomedes. Or great Agamemnon himself. Zeus, let it be a worthy champion!"

Their prayers were answered. The stone that came out of the helmet carried the mark of Ajax of Salamis. He was delighted.

"Pray for me while I put on my armour!" he called to the soldiers.

So the troops went on praying, looking up into the sky. "Father Zeus, let Ajax win. Or, if you love Hector too much to let him be defeated, then may the fight be drawn. But don't let Ajax be beaten!"

Inspired by their prayers Ajax took up his shield and marched out to meet Hector. "Now you'll see what it's like to face a true Greek warrior!" he said. "Achilles may be out of the battle, for now, but there are still plenty of us who can match you, Trojan. Defend yourself!"

Hector raised his head and his helmet flashed in the sun. "You won't scare me with words. I grew up with a spear in my hand. Take guard – invader!"

He threw his long javelin, with all the power in his body. Ajax caught the weapon on his shield, but the point sliced through its bronze surface, cutting deep into the leather behind. The impact threw him backwards.

Recovering his balance, he flung his own spear, even harder. Hector swerved sideways, thrusting out his shield – and Ajax's spear went right through it, ripping the side of Hector's tunic. If he hadn't dodged quickly, he would have been dead.

The two men fell on each other like two wild boars. Ajax's spear grazed Hector's neck, drawing blood. In reply, Hector snatched up a jagged boulder and threw it so hard that it made Ajax's shield clang like a bell.

Ajax threw an even bigger rock. It dented Hector's shield and knocked him off his feet, but he jumped up immediately. Drawing his sword, he ran at Ajax.

They fought until the sun went down and the light began to fail. Then heralds came running out from the two armies.

"You're both great warriors," they shouted. "Zeus loves you both too much to see you hacking at each other in the dark."

Ajax lowered his sword. "Hector challenged me to fight. Is he ready to stop?"

"You're a mighty warrior," Hector answered. "But we can hardly see each other. Let us stop for today, and exchange gifts to show our respect for each other." He held out his silver-studded sword to Ajax.

Ajax accepted the sword and gave Hector his magnificent purple belt. Then, as night fell, the Greeks went back to their ships and the Trojans retreated inside the city walls.

PARIS MAKES AN OFFER AND THE GREEKS MAKE A WALL

THE TROJANS WERE RELIEVED to see Hector come back safely, but they longed for an end to the war. Their leaders gathered together in King Priam's palace and one of them, called Antenor, dared to say aloud what many were thinking.

"What are we fighting for?" he said. "This is not an honourable war for us. We should give Helen back to Menelaus – with all her treasure."

Paris jumped to his feet, shouting furiously. "Helen is my wife! I will never let her go! But I don't care about the treasure. Menelaus can have it all – and more besides – if he agrees to end the war and go away."

Other people began to shout, some agreeing with Paris and some with Antenor. King Priam stood, raising his hands for silence.

"Paris has made a fair offer," he said. "Tomorrow morning, let's send Idaeus, our herald, to the Greek ships, to tell Agamemnon and Menelaus what Paris says. At the same time, he can ask for a truce, to let us carry our dead warriors from the battlefield and give them a proper funeral."

Everyone agreed to this plan. They all went off to their separate quarters, hopeful that the end of the war was in sight at last.

In the Greek camp, there was a completely different mood. Ajax was welcomed as though he'd won a great victory. Agamemnon had a fine bull roasted, and he carved the best pieces of meat for Ajax.

As the Greek kings sat together after the feast, wise old Nestor leaned forward into the firelight.

"I have a plan," he said. "Many of our brave soldiers have been killed, and their bodies are scattered across the plain. Let's arrange a truce tomorrow morning, so that we can retrieve the bodies and build a funeral pyre."

Everyone agreed with that. But Nestor hadn't finished.

"We can use the funeral pyre to build a defence for our ships. After the bodies are burnt, we can pile earth on top of the pyre to make a long mound, sealing off this beach. If we put wooden walls on top of the mound and dig a trench in front of it, our ships will be well protected."

The other kings liked Nestor's plan – and soon they were given a chance to carry it out. Before sunrise next morning, the Trojan herald

Idaeus arrived, bringing the message from King Priam.

"Noble lords," he said, "I have come to ask for a truce. We want to give our dead heroes a proper funeral. Also, I bring you a generous offer from Prince Paris. If you agree to end this unhappy war, he'll give back all the treasure he took from Sparta – with more besides, from his own treasure store. But he insists on keeping Helen as his wife."

The Greek kings stared back at him. They were stunned.

"We can't accept!" Diomedes said fiercely. "Not even if he offers to give up Helen too. We're going to win this war!"

The other kings roared their agreement and Agamemnon turned to the herald. "You've heard our answer," he said. "The war goes on. But we will agree to a truce today. Go back and tell Priam that he can collect the bodies of his soldiers. We'll do the same."

By the time the sun rose, Greeks and Trojans were out on the battlefield again. They came face to face with each other, but there was no fighting this time. Instead, they searched for their dead comrades, solemnly loading their bodies on to wagons. The Trojans built a funeral pyre outside the city walls. The Greeks made theirs across the entrance to the harbour.

All day, the sky was dark with smoke and there was deep sadness on both sides of the plain.

Before dawn the next morning, the Greeks gathered secretly, beside the cold remains of their funeral pyre. Working in the dark, they

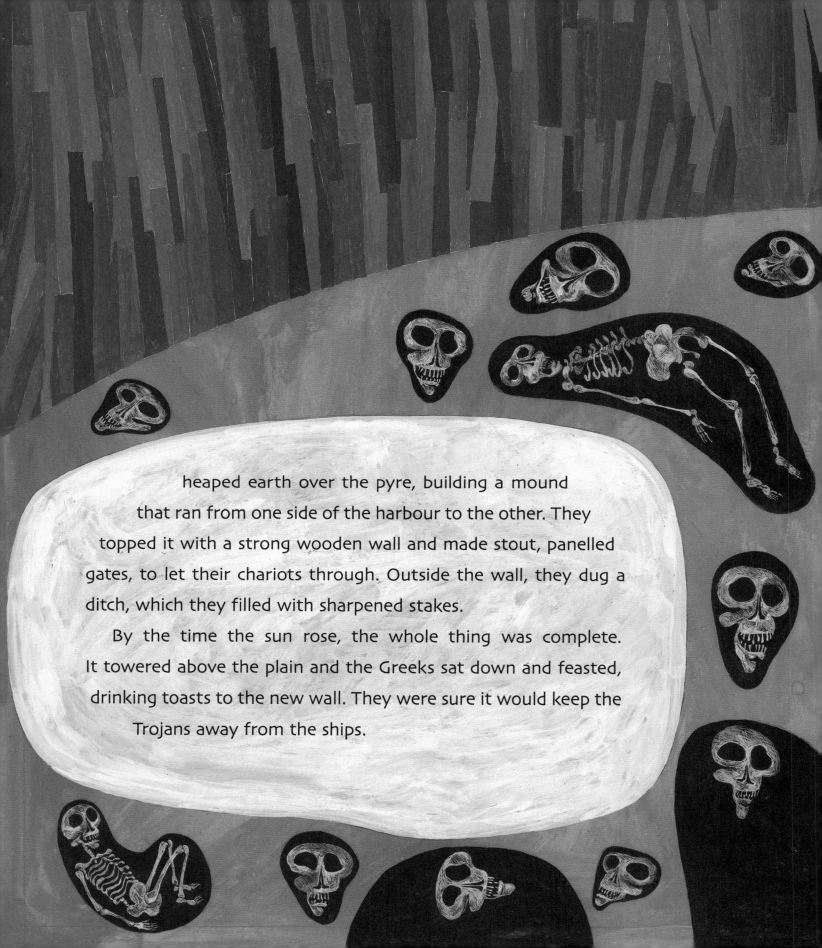

heaped earth over the pyre, building a mound
that ran from one side of the harbour to the other. They
topped it with a strong wooden wall and made stout, panelled
gates, to let their chariots through. Outside the wall, they dug a
ditch, which they filled with sharpened stakes.

By the time the sun rose, the whole thing was complete.
It towered above the plain and the Greeks sat down and feasted,
drinking toasts to the new wall. They were sure it would keep the
Trojans away from the ships.

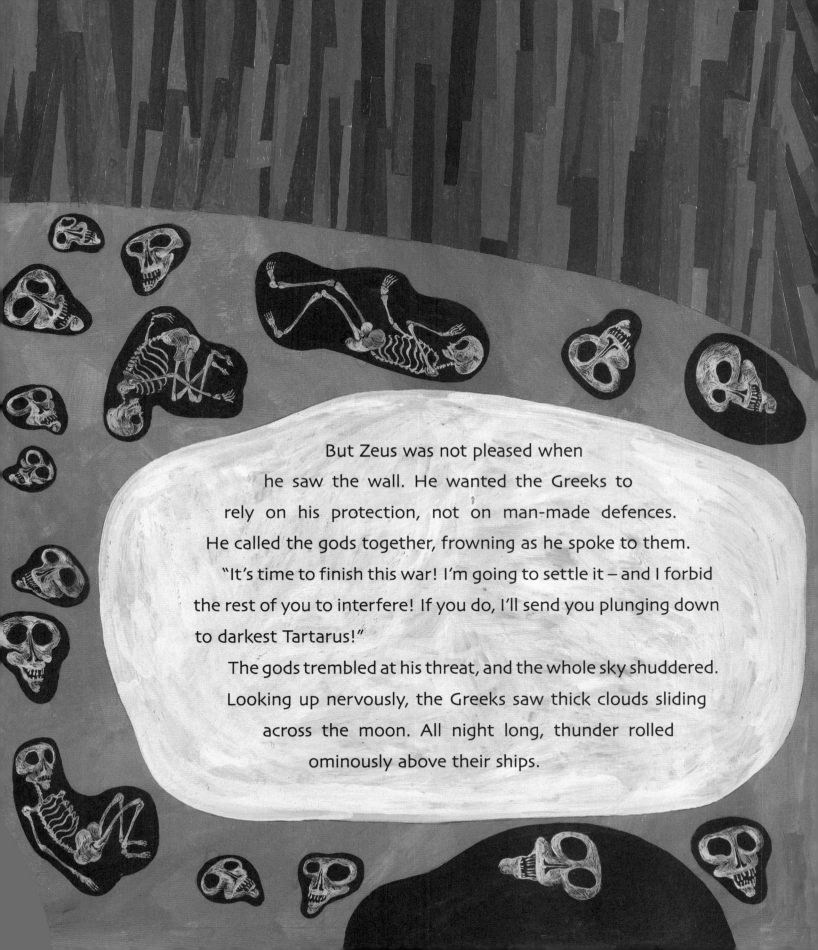

But Zeus was not pleased when
he saw the wall. He wanted the Greeks to
rely on his protection, not on man-made defences.
He called the gods together, frowning as he spoke to them.

"It's time to finish this war! I'm going to settle it – and I forbid
the rest of you to interfere! If you do, I'll send you plunging down
to darkest Tartarus!"

The gods trembled at his threat, and the whole sky shuddered.
Looking up nervously, the Greeks saw thick clouds sliding
across the moon. All night long, thunder rolled
ominously above their ships.

GREEKS ON THE RUN

|||||||||||||||||||||||||||||||||||||||||||||||||||||||||||||||||||||||||||||||||

NEXT MORNING, Zeus watched as the two armies woke and prepared to fight. At sunrise, the Greek chariots charged through the strong new gates and down on to the plain. Immediately, the Trojan chariots flew out of the city to meet them.

Metal clashed as the two armies met and the soldiers bellowed their war-cries at each other. Soon, screams rang across the plain and the earth was red with blood. Neither army would give ground.

But, at midday, Zeus took out his golden scales and held them high. Into one pan he put death for the Trojans. Into the other – death for the Greeks. Holding the balance steady, he waited to see which death carried more weight.

Slowly, inexorably, the Trojan side rose into the air and the Greek side sank down towards the earth .

Zeus acted at once. His thunder rolled over the Greek army and he

sent a flash of lightning slicing down among its soldiers. The Greeks were terrified.

They knew at once that Zeus was against them and they lost all hope of winning that day. Turning their chariots towards the ships, they raced back to safety behind their new wall.

But old Nestor couldn't retreat. Paris had shot one of his chariot horses in the head. The poor animal was writhing round and round, thrashing out with its hooves as it tried to dislodge the arrow. Nestor was left all on his own, stranded in the middle of the battlefield.

Jumping out of his chariot, he slashed at the wounded animal's reins, trying to cut the other horses free. Hector saw him and seized the chance to attack. He snatched the reins from his charioteer and turned his own horses quickly, urging them across the battlefield. With his other hand, he held his spear up, ready to strike.

Diomedes spotted what was happening. He shouted an order to his charioteer and they turned and raced towards Nestor. As he went, Diomedes bellowed to Odysseus.

"Stop running away! Nestor needs our help! We must save him from that Trojan savage!"

He was wasting his breath. Odysseus couldn't hear him above the turmoil of the battlefield. Diomedes realized that he would have to save Nestor on his own. Sweeping towards the old king's chariot, he called down to him.

"Leave the charioteers to cut your horses free while we go and deal with Hector. We'll teach him a lesson!"

Diomedes' charioteer jumped down and Nestor leapt eagerly into his place. Taking up the reins, he turned the horses round, with Diomedes beside him, ready to attack. As soon as they were near enough, Diomedes threw his spear at Hector's charioteer, killing him instantly.

Hector was devastated to see his charioteer fall to the ground. But there was no time to mourn. Diomedes and Nestor were heading towards him at top speed. Snatching at the reins, he pulled his horses to a stop and yelled for someone else to come and drive his chariot.

Diomedes' chariot swung round. He was ready to attack again, but Zeus had other plans. There was a terrifying clap of thunder, and a bolt of lightning hit the ground, right in front of Diomedes' horses. They shied and skittered back, and Nestor dropped the reins in terror.

"Zeus is against us!" he shouted. "We must get back to the ships. We don't stand a chance of winning today."

Diomedes was horrified. "You're asking me to run away? From *Hector*? Do you want him to call us cowards?"

"Who cares what he calls us? Everyone knows you're not a coward." Nestor picked up the reins again and turned the horses, sending the chariot racing towards the shore.

Hector gave a triumphant roar. "You're a weakling, Diomedes! A rag doll! I'll see you down in Hades, with the dead, before you break into Troy!"

Diomedes grabbed at the reins. He would have pulled the chariot round and charged at Hector, but a second crack of thunder made him think again. Dropping his hand, he let Nestor whip up the horses. They raced back to the wall, with the Trojan chariots close behind them.

Galloping through the gates, they found themselves in a wild tangle of horses and harness. The Greek chariots were crammed in between the ships, and the soldiers were scurrying round in a panic. They thought the Trojans would come sweeping in through the gates before there was time to pull them shut.

Agamemnon jumped on to the prow of Odysseus' ship, holding a great purple cloak. He waved it in the air, to catch everyone's attention.

"Shame on you all!" he yelled. "When we first came here, you boasted about how many Trojans you were going to kill. What's happened to all that spirit? Are you going to let our enemies overrun the beach, without even trying to fight back?"

He lifted his arms to heaven, calling out desperately to Zeus.

"Mighty Father, remember all the sacrifices I have made to you and hear my prayer! Save our lives!"

Zeus did hear him, and he sent a sign. A huge eagle came flying overhead, carrying a young deer. As it flew over the Greek camp, the eagle dropped the deer, right next to the altar where Agamemnon made his sacrifices to Zeus.

When they saw that, the Greeks turned to fight again. They attacked so fiercely that the Trojans were driven away from the wall and back across the trench. Hastily the gates were closed and barred behind them.

For that night, at least, the Greek army was safe.

But Hector knew he had the upper hand – and he didn't mean to lose it. He wouldn't allow his soldiers to retreat into the city. Instead, he told some of them to collect firewood and sent others back into Troy to fetch supplies. He ordered them to make camp out on the plain, between the city and the Greek ships.

That night, a thousand campfires burned on the battlefield. The air was filled with the crackle of flames and the smell of roasting meat. Fifty men feasted around each campfire. Beside their chariots, the horses stood ready, munching barley and rye to give them strength for the next day.

Hemmed in behind the wall, the Greeks could hear their enemies rejoicing. They were filled with fear as they looked across at the red glow of the campfires, drowning out the stars.

PLEADING WITH ACHILLES

AGAMEMNON SAW A TRAP CLOSING round his army. He was ready to abandon the whole war.

"Zeus is against us," he said to the other kings. "That means the Trojans are going to win. Let's sail home now, or they'll burn our ships and we'll be left at their mercy."

Diomedes was outraged. "Where's your courage? We're not all cowards. You can sail home if you like. The rest of us will stay here – and capture Troy!"

There were cheers from all the others and Nestor nodded wisely.

"This is a crucial night," he said. "And you must give a lead, Lord Agamemnon. Let's sit down and discuss what to do."

Agamemnon took Nestor's advice. He posted sentries around the camp and then called the Greek kings together for a council of war.

Nestor spoke first and he was very blunt. "We all know why the Trojans are overrunning us," he said to Agamemnon. "It's your fault,

53

for snatching Briseis away from Achilles. He's our best warrior and we'll never win without him. You have to apologize for what you did and send peace offerings."

"You're right," Agamemnon said ruefully. "I must have been out of my mind to quarrel with him. If he agrees to join us again, I'll send Briseis straight back to him, with a heap of treasure. And when we get home I'll give him seven fine towns and let him choose one of my daughters as his wife."

Nestor nodded. "That's very generous. Let's send Odysseus and Ajax to tell Achilles what you've said."

He knew Odysseus would persuade Achilles – if anyone could.

Ajax and Odysseus set out immediately, walking down the line of ships to the far end, where Achilles and the Myrmidons had built their huts. As they approached Achilles' hut, they heard the sound of a lute, and a man's voice singing about ancient heroes.

The singer was Achilles. He and his friend Patroclus were sitting on chairs in front of the hut and when they saw Odysseus and Ajax, they jumped up to greet them.

"Welcome!" said Achilles. "I may be angry, but it's still good to see you two. I wondered when someone would come." He ushered them into the hut and offered them food and wine.

Odysseus came straight to the point. "We're faced with disaster. Unless you help us, the Trojans will break through our wall and burn the ships. Agamemnon is ready to make peace with you. If you agree to fight again, he'll send Briseis back. He'll give you a pile of treasure too, and seven fine towns. And you can marry whichever of his daughters you like."

"I'm not interested in Agamemnon's daughters," Achilles said angrily. "Or his treasure. When he stole Briseis, he insulted me. Why should I risk being killed to rescue his brother's wife?"

"How can you be so arrogant?" said Ajax. "Don't you care about the Greek soldiers? You know they idolize you."

"Of course I care," Achilles said. "But I can't forgive Agamemnon. Go back and tell him that I won't fight – not unless Hector burns the Greek ships and fights his way to the door of my hut. In fact, I'm thinking of sailing home tomorrow."

Odysseus and Ajax could see they were never going to persuade him. Unhappily they walked back along the shore to Agamemnon's hut. When he saw them coming, he jumped up.

"Well?" he asked eagerly. "What did Achilles say?"

Odysseus shook his head. "He won't change his mind, whatever you offer him. He's threatening to leave us and sail back to Greece. Don't waste any more time thinking about him. Let's go and sleep. We need to be ready for the fight tomorrow."

SPIES

||||||||||||||||||||||||||||||||||||||||||||||||||||||||||||||||||

AGAMEMNON KNEW ODYSSEUS WAS RIGHT. But even though he went to bed, he couldn't sleep. He tossed and turned, thinking about the campfires just beyond the wall.

Was it really sensible to stay and fight? What would they do if the Trojans launched a night attack?

Wouldn't it be wiser to hurry aboard their ships and sail away while they still had the chance?

At last he dressed and went outside, to wander round the camp. He checked the sentries and then called the other leaders together for a midnight council.

They gathered outside, on the very spot where the Trojans had turned back the evening before. Nestor looked out at the campfires burning on the plain.

"A brave man could sneak across there," he said slowly. "He might even be able to listen to what the Trojans are saying."

There was a long silence.

Then Diomedes said, "I'll go. Will anyone come with me?"

At once, several others stepped forward.

"Choose someone," said Agamemnon.

"I'll take Odysseus," Diomedes said quickly. "I'd go through fire with him. And his brain moves even faster than his sword."

"Don't waste time flattering me," muttered Odysseus. "Let's go, before it gets too light."

Before they went, they disguised themselves in borrowed helmets. Odysseus wore one belonging to Meriones, decorated with boars' tusks and Diomedes pulled on a young warrior's leather skullcap. Then, like lions slinking through the darkness, they crept across the plain, picking their way between the bodies of dead soldiers.

They weren't the only spies sent out that night. Hector had had the same idea as Nestor. He offered a rich reward to any Trojan who would sneak over the wall and spy on the Greek ships.

At first, no one dared to volunteer. Finally one of the Trojan heralds stepped forward – an ugly man called Dolon.

"I'll go," he said. "But I want a reward when we've conquered the Greeks. Promise that you'll give me Achilles' chariot. And his immortal horses."

"No other Trojan shall ride behind those horses," said Hector.

(If only he'd been able to look into the future! If only he'd guessed

which Trojan would really travel behind Achilles' horses! But he didn't know what he was saying.)

Dolon disguised himself in a wolfskin cloak and a cap of fur. Slipping away from the Trojan camp, he ran across the battlefield, towards the Greek wall.

But he moved clumsily and Odysseus saw him coming.

"Look, there's a Trojan spy," he whispered to Diomedes. "As soon as he's gone past, let's grab him from behind."

Diomedes nodded. They turned off the path and crouched down among the bodies of the dead. Dolon ran by without seeing them and they jumped up and started chasing him.

When he heard them, he tried to circle back to the Trojan camp. But Diomedes and Odysseus split up, one going left and one right, heading him off like sheepdogs. As they approached the Greek sentries, Diomedes put on a spurt.

"Stop!" he yelled at Dolon. "Or you're a dead man!"

As he shouted, he threw his spear, aiming deliberately high. The spear whistled over Dolon's shoulder and he skidded to a stop. When Odysseus and Diomedes seized him, he burst into tears.

"Don't kill me!" he babbled. "Please don't kill me! My father will give you a good ransom if you send me back alive. I'm not really a spy! It's all Hector's fault. He bribed me. He said he would give me Achilles' chariot and his horses."

Odysseus smiled grimly at the thought of such a coward driving

Achilles' immortal horses. "We're not interested in you," he snapped. "We want to know about the Trojan troops."

Immediately, Dolon blurted out everything he knew. He told them exactly where all the different units were camped. "The Thracians are nearest," he said. "And Rhesus, their king, has some wonderful horses. They're fast and white and beautiful. Why don't you steal them? If you let me go—"

"If we let you go, you'll spy on us again," Diomedes said shortly. "There's only one way to stop you making trouble." He swung his sword suddenly and Dolon's head flew off his body and thudded to the ground. Diomedes and Odysseus stripped off his armour and hid it in a bush. Then they crept on, towards the Trojan camp.

Everything was exactly as Dolon had described. The Thracians were sleeping peacefully beside their horses. As Odysseus and Diomedes lifted their swords, King Rhesus was in the middle of a nightmare – about Diomedes. He woke up suddenly and found that his dream was true. The nightmare figure was there, looming over him.

A second later, he was dead.

Odysseus ran to untie the horses and Diomedes moved through the camp, swinging his sword again and again. He had killed a dozen more Thracians by the time Odysseus

whistled, to show that he was ready. He and Diomedes leapt on to two of the horses, and galloped away across the plain, taking the others with them.

They left just in time. As they rode away, the rest of the Thracians woke up. They stared round in horror at their dead comrades and the empty space where the horses had been.

Odysseus and Diomedes paused for a second, to snatch up Dolon's armour, and then galloped furiously towards the ships. Before the first light of dawn, they had reached the earth wall and the sentries were opening the gates to let them through.

When the Greeks saw the splendid horses they'd brought back, they were filled with new confidence. All at once, they were keen to fight the Trojans again.

DISASTER FOR THE GREEKS

||||||||||||||||||||||||||||||||||||||||||||||||||||||||||||||||||||||

NEXT MORNING, both armies strode out to meet each other. The soldiers swung their blades like reapers cutting corn and Agamemnon fought as fiercely as a lion.

"Push forward!" he shouted to his men. "As hard as you can!"

Gradually the Trojans were forced back towards the Scaean gate. Now the Greeks were close to the walls of Troy. It looked as though they were on the brink of victory at last.

But the war wasn't destined to end yet. As the Trojans huddled together outside their gates, Zeus sent Iris, the rainbow goddess, to encourage Hector.

"Be brave!" she told him. "I bring a message from Zeus. He says that you should order your men to keep fighting, but hold back yourself – until Agamemnon is wounded. When that happens, and you see him withdraw from the fight, charge forward and attack the Greeks as hard as you can. If you do that, you'll reach their ships before nightfall."

She vanished, and Hector turned to his troops. "Keep fighting!" he shouted. "Zeus has promised us victory!"

As Zeus had ordered, he held back from the fighting himself. He watched Agamemnon charge towards the Trojans and saw a young man called Iphidamas step out to meet him.

Iphidamas had left home on his wedding day to help with the defence of Troy. But he was no match for Agamemnon. As they clashed, his spear buckled against the Greek king's shield – and that was the end of him.

He lay dead on the battlefield and his young wife never saw him again.

Iphidamas' brother, Coön, saw him fall and he flung himself furiously at Agamemnon. Within seconds he was dead too. But before he died he slashed at Agamemnon with his spear and wounded the Greek king's arm.

It wasn't a death wound, but when the arm began to stiffen, it was so painful that Agamemnon was forced to leave the battle. Jumping into his chariot, he called on the other Greeks to keep fighting while he went back to the ships.

Hector's moment had come. In a great voice, he shouted to the Trojan army. "Agamemnon is running away! Fight like men! Zeus gives us victory!"

He roared out on to the battlefield, with all the Trojans behind him. The Greeks began to fall back, retreating towards the ships.

Odysseus saw what was happening. "We must hold the Trojans back!" he called to Diomedes. "If Hector captures our ships, we lose everything. Come here and make a stand with me."

Diomedes raced across to him and the two heroes stood shoulder to shoulder, blocking the Trojans' way. Even Hector couldn't make them run. As he approached, Diomedes threw a spear that hit him on the helmet. The blow was so hard it almost knocked Hector unconscious. He just managed to stagger back into his chariot.

As he escaped, Diomedes bellowed after him. "You've saved your skin this time! But next time I'll finish you off!"

He didn't realize that Paris was very close, hiding behind a wall. As Diomedes shouted, Paris sneaked out and shot at him. The arrow pierced Diomedes' foot, pinning it to the ground.

Paris stepped clear of his hiding place and began to gloat. "How does it feel to be wounded, Diomedes? It's a pity you're not dead!"

"It's only a scratch, Mr Pretty Hair!" Diomedes yelled back. "If you were a real man, you'd have come out to meet me face to face. With a real weapon!"

He sounded ferocious, but they were empty words. To free himself, he had to pull out Paris's arrow. When he did, the pain was unbearable. He had to climb into his chariot and head back to the ships.

That left Odysseus on his own, facing the whole Trojan army. The Trojans surrounded him, like hunters circling a wild boar. He kept fighting bravely and managed to kill some of them, but finally a spear went right through his shield and into his side.

The Trojans would have slaughtered him then, but Menelaus and Ajax came to his rescue. Fighting their way through to him, they hoisted him into his chariot and sent it back behind the wall.

Paris was still skulking in his hiding place, shooting at every Greek he could reach. One of his arrows hit Machaon, the doctor who treated the wounded Greeks. Nestor knew it would be a disaster if Machaon died, so he went racing to the rescue. But that took Nestor out of the battle too. Once he had lifted Machaon into his chariot, he had to take him back to the ships.

Achilles watched everything from behind the wall. When he saw the Greeks retreating, he was triumphant.

"They'll come and grovel to me now," he told Patroclus. He leaned forward as Nestor's chariot caught his eye. "That looks like Machaon, the doctor, riding with Nestor. Is he wounded? Go and find out, Patroclus."

Obediently Patroclus set out along the beach. He found Machaon in Nestor's hut. He and Nestor were drinking wine and eating barley pottage.

"Come in!" Nestor said.

Patroclus shook his head. "I must go straight back to Achilles. He wants to know if Machaon is injured."

"It's not only Machaon," Nestor said bitterly. "Diomedes is wounded too, and so is Odysseus. And Greeks are dying all over the battlefield. But your precious master won't do anything to help."

Patroclus was horrified, but Nestor didn't stop.

"You're just as bad!" he said. "Why don't you tell Achilles what's happening? Tell him he has to fight! And if he won't – borrow his armour and lead the Myrmidons yourself!"

By then, Patroclus was almost in tears. He ran out of Nestor's hut and headed back along the line of ships. But, before he reached Achilles' hut, he met another wounded man. A soldier called Eurypylus was dragging himself across the beach, with an arrow in his thigh.

Patroclus understood, at last, that the whole army was on the verge of death and disaster.

"Is everything lost?" he called to Eurypylus. "Are we defeated?"

"No one can hold Hector back," gasped Eurypylus. "The Trojans are sweeping towards our wall – and there's no one to help the wounded. You know something about healing, don't you? Please cut this arrow out of my leg."

How could Patroclus say no? He knew Achilles was waiting impatiently for him, but he couldn't ignore Eurypylus. He helped him back to his hut and laid him gently on the ground. Then, deftly and carefully, he cut out the head of the arrow. When it was gone, he dressed the wound with a poultice of herbs, holding it in place to try and stop the bleeding.

While Patroclus was looking after Eurypylus, the Trojans began another fierce assault. This time, they attacked on foot.

Hector realized that their chariots would never make it across the trench, so he leapt to the ground, calling on the other nobles to follow him. Joining the foot soldiers, they charged down into the trench and up the other side, brandishing their weapons as they flung themselves at the wall.

The Greeks threw huge rocks down on to them, but the Trojans replied by hurling bigger stones at the wall. They flew like snow in a blizzard, clanging against helmets and shields and covering the ground.

Then Zeus sent a sign.

An eagle flew over the Trojan army, carrying a blood-red snake in its beak. Suddenly, the snake twisted round and bit the eagle's neck.

The eagle dropped it and flew away and the snake lay writhing on the ground, in the middle of the Trojan army.

It was a terrible omen. The Trojans were appalled.

But Hector refused to retreat. "Zeus has promised us victory!" he shouted. "Today we're going to reach the enemy's ships. Forward!" He ran at the wall and, with a great roar, his men charged after him, hacking into the wood.

The Greeks defended doggedly, blocking each gap as it opened up and slashing at the Trojans across the battlements. But Hector was relentless.

"Victory is in sight!" he bellowed. "Break down the wall and burn the ships!"

Seizing an enormous rock, he launched himself at the panelled gates that barred their way. He flung the rock so hard that it broke the hinges of both gates, smashing their panels to firewood.

The Trojans were through the wall!

With a cry of triumph, Hector scrambled over the broken gates. His eyes flamed and his whole body was blazing with the fire of battle. As the Trojans flooded after him, the Greeks fled in a panic, scurrying between the ships for shelter.

THE GODS INTERFERE

THE GODS who supported the Greeks were furious and frustrated. Zeus had ordered them not to interfere, but they couldn't bear to stand by and see the Greeks defeated.

So they plotted to get Zeus out of the way. Hera, his wife, lured him into their bedroom, whispering, "I want to be alone with you." Once he was off guard, she lulled him to sleep, so that he wouldn't see what was happening.

As soon as Zeus's eyes closed, his brother, Poseidon, raced down from Olympus, striding over the mountain tops until he reached the Greek ships. He disguised himself as the prophet Calchas and went to find Ajax.

"Make a stand against Hector!" he said. "If you dare to face him, others will come to join you." He reached out his staff and fired Ajax with new courage. Then he disappeared.

That wasn't Calchas, Ajax thought. *It was one of the immortal gods!*

71

He seized his weapons boldly and turned to face the Trojans. And one by one, as Poseidon spoke to them, the other Greeks came to join him until he was standing at the centre of a long hedge of spears and shields.

The Trojans thundered through the Greek camp towards them. Hector was leading the way. When his soldiers saw the line of armed men, they stopped in amazement.

"Keep going!" Hector shouted.

Bronze armour flashed as the two lines met. They were so evenly matched that neither side gave way. The Greeks couldn't drive the Trojans back and – however hard he tried – Hector couldn't break through to the ships.

But Agamemnon was watching, with the other wounded kings. He saw how close the Trojans were, and he knew what would happen if they did get past Ajax. *They would set the ships on fire.*

Then the Greeks would be trapped between the wall and the sea. The Trojans would slaughter them all.

Agamemnon panicked. "We must launch the ships!" he said to Odysseus and Diomedes. "We must sail to safety – before it's too late!"

Odysseus stared at him. "You want us to run away? After all we've been through? What kind of king are you? Anyway, it's impossible. The Trojans will cut us down before we can pull the ships into the water."

"We shouldn't be planning a retreat!" Diomedes said fiercely. "We

HE SAW HOW CLOSE THE TROJANS WERE AND HE KNEW WHAT WOULD HAPPEN IF THEY DID GET PAST AJAX.

BUT AGAMEMNON WAS WATCHING WITH THE OTHER WOUNDED KINGS

HE TROJANS THUNDERED THROUGH E GREEK CAMP TOWARDS THEM. HECTOR WAS ADING THE WAY. WHEN HIS SOLDIERS SAW THE LINE ARMED MEN, THEY STOPPED IN AMAZEMENT. KEEP GOING!" HECTOR SHOUTED.

BRONZE ARMOUR FLASHED AS THE TWO LINES MET. THEY WERE SO EVENLY MATCHED THAT NEITHER SIDE GAVE WAY. THE GREEKS COULDN'T DRIVE THE TROJANS BACK AND-HOWEVER HARD HE TRIED HECTOR COULDN'T BREAK THROUGH TO THE SHIPS.

should be out there in the battle. I know we can't fight ourselves, but we can encourage the others."

Agamemnon realized they were right. Quickly the three wounded kings went towards the battle. When they appeared, the Greek soldiers rallied, attacking the Trojans again. Poseidon was still there, urging them on, and slowly the Trojans began to give ground. The Greeks advanced, pressing them hard.

And Ajax and Hector came face to face for the second time.

Hector reacted instantly, with a spear that flew straight and true. It hit Ajax, but it glanced off his armour without doing any harm.

Ajax responded by flinging a massive rock, as hard as he could. It hit Hector on the chest, above his shield, and knocked him to the ground.

That changed everything. Hector lay on his back, panting and spitting blood, and the horrified Trojans turned and ran back over the wall. It looked as though the Greeks had won.

But then Zeus woke up and saw what was happening.

And he was furious.

"What have you done?" he thundered, turning on Hera. "I made a promise to Thetis and I mean to keep it. No victory for the Greeks until the insult to Achilles is avenged!"

Thunder rolled over the rocks of high Olympus and dark clouds covered the sky above as he roared out orders to Iris and Apollo. They obeyed instantly, racing down to Troy to change the course of the battle. Iris went to stop Poseidon interfering and Apollo appeared beside Hector, who was still on the ground, half stunned.

"On your feet!" said Apollo. "Call up your chariots! Zeus has sent me to help you."

Immediately Hector leapt up, full of new energy. The Greeks were horrified. They'd thought he was dead, but there he was, ordering another attack. Within minutes, the Trojan chariots were pouring through the gates and the Greeks were driven back helplessly towards their ships.

PATROCLUS IN DISGUISE

||||||||||||||||||||||||||||||||||||||||||||||||||||||

PATROCLUS WAS STILL LOOKING AFTER EURYPYLUS. Hearing the thunder of hooves, he looked out of the hut and saw Trojan chariots flooding over the wall.

He jumped up. "I can't stay here!" he said. "I must go back and persuade Achilles to fight – before it's too late!" He left Eurypylus and raced back along the beach, as the Greeks lost even more ground.

Now the Trojans were almost at the ships.

Ajax was in the front line, fighting the hardest battle of his life. But he knew he couldn't keep the Trojans away from the ships with his normal weapons. He needed something much bigger. Something extraordinary. Like—

Suddenly, he saw how to do it.

Stepping back from the battle line, he scrambled aboard one of the ships. On the deck was a great pole, over twelve metres long. Heaving it up, he swung it furiously at the approaching Trojans. It knocked a dozen of them off their feet.

Exultantly, Ajax swung the pole again, leaping from ship to ship like a trick rider changing horses. "Don't give up!" he shouted to the Greeks. "We must drive them back!"

But Hector was shouting too, bellowing above the noise of the battle. Dodging Ajax's pole, he managed to struggle right up to one of the ships. He caught hold of its wooden side, clinging on tightly.

"Zeus is with us!" he yelled. "The ships are ours! BRING FIRE!"

The Trojans ran at the ships with blazing torches. Desperately, Ajax swung his pole again, trying to knock them back. As he swung, he shouted a last, desperate appeal to the Greeks.

"Show that you're men!" he bellowed. "There are no allies to come and rescue us. No other walls to protect us. We have to save ourselves! Fight for your lives!"

The words thundered across the beach, echoing round Patroclus as he raced to Achilles' hut. By the time he reached it, he was weeping and gasping for breath.

Achilles jumped up and ran to meet him.

"What's the matter?" he called.

Patroclus pointed towards the battle, covering his face.

"Don't be such a baby," Achilles said scornfully. "Why should you care about those miserable Greeks? They deserve it!"

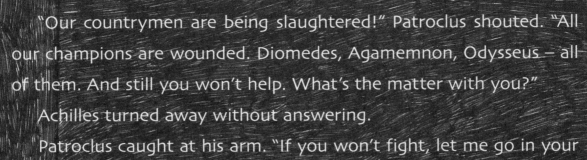

"Our countrymen are being slaughtered!" Patroclus shouted. "All our champions are wounded. Diomedes, Agamemnon, Odysseus – all of them. And still you won't help. What's the matter with you?"

Achilles turned away without answering.

Patroclus caught at his arm. "If you won't fight, let me go in your place. I can borrow your armour and lead the Myrmidons into battle. If the Trojans think it's you, they may give up and retreat."

That tore at Achilles' heart. "You know what the matter is!" he cried. "I've been treated like a beggar! Agamemnon – who's no better than I am – used his power to rob me of Briseis. I want to see him beaten and grovelling, so that my honour is restored. But now the Trojans are here – and how can I let them burn the ships?"

He looked along the beach and saw the Myrmidons standing outside their huts. They were all staring at the battle, and he knew they were aching to be there.

Slowly he turned back to Patroclus. "You can take my armour," he said. "You can lead the Myrmidons out, and drive Hector back over the wall. But when that's done – come back to me. *Don't go on towards Troy on your own.*"

As he spoke, there was a clatter of stones from further down the shore. Ajax was still swinging at the Trojans, but now they were replying with rocks. He was holding his shield up on one arm, to fend them off, but he looked exhausted.

Hector darted in suddenly, slashing at the giant pole. It snapped off and Ajax was left with a useless stump in his hand. The Trojans surged forward, yelling triumphantly and throwing their lighted torches on to the deck. Ajax only just had time to jump clear before the ship caught fire.

Achilles saw the flames shooting up into the sky. "Fetch my armour, Patroclus!" he shouted. "I'll call the men together while you put it on."

Patroclus snatched up the bronze greaves and fastened them round his legs. Quickly he buckled on the shining breast-plate and slung the sword and shield on straps over his shoulders. Then he lifted Achilles' well-known helmet, with its great horsehair plume.

Once the helmet was on, most of his face was hidden. Anyone who saw him now would think he was Achilles.

He seized two spears – but not the longest, which only Achilles could manage. Then he shouted to Automedon, the charioteer, ordering him to harness Achilles' beautiful horses.

Xanthus and Balius were no ordinary horses. Their mother had mated with the West Wind himself and they were immortal. They pawed at the ground and tossed their heads, eager to join the fight.

84

Achilles was storming along the beach, calling the Myrmidons. They lined up instantly, as eager as the horses. There were five companies, each of five hundred men, as loyal and savage as mountain wolves.

"I know you have been longing to join the battle!" Achilles shouted. "This is your chance! Go and show the Trojans how to fight!"

The Myrmidons stood shoulder to shoulder, with their spears held ready and their shields in a solid wall. Ordering his chariot to the front, Patroclus raised a hand and waved them forward. With a clash of bronze and a thunder of tramping feet, they headed for the Trojan army.

Going back into his hut, Achilles opened a beautiful inlaid chest. He took out a special cup and filled it with wine. Then he went outside to pray. Looking up to the sky, he poured the wine on to the ground as an offering.

"Father Zeus," he prayed, "give Patroclus victory over the Trojans. Let him drive them back from the ships and over the wall! Then bring him back here safely, with every one of the soldiers and all his armour."

Looking down from high Olympus, Zeus listened to Achilles' prayer.

And he granted half of it.

PATROCLUS MEETS HIS FATE

||||||||||||||||||||||||||||||||||||||||||||||||||||||

URGED ON BY SHOUTS FROM PATROCLUS, the Myrmidons charged along the shore, like wasps pouring out of a nest.

"Show your courage!" Patroclus yelled. "Bring glory to Achilles! Let Agamemnon know what a fool he was to insult him!"

Bellowing their terrible war-cry, the Myrmidons launched themselves into battle. The noise echoed around the ships, filling the Trojans with terror. They were even more terrified when they saw the man who led the charge, standing tall behind the immortal horses. As the sun gleamed on his beautiful bronze armour, they were sure they were looking at the great Achilles himself.

Patroclus drove straight to the blazing ship. He put out the flames and the Greeks leaped from their hiding places. They thought Achilles was with them – and they were eager to fight again.

87

Slowly the Trojans were forced back, away from the ships. Hector tried to keep them together, giving ground gradually, but when they saw the gleaming figure in Achilles' armour all their courage vanished. They turned and fled, running away from the ships and back across the wall.

Patroclus had saved the Greeks from disaster. Once he saw the Trojans retreating he should have obeyed Achilles' orders and turned back. If he'd done that, he would have been a hero, and lived to fight another day.

But he was drunk on dreams of glory and he forgot what Achilles had said. All he could think of was killing Hector – and maybe even breaking into Troy itself.

"Drive on!" he shouted to the charioteer.

The immortal horses galloped through the gates and leapt straight over the trench. As they charged across the plain, the Trojans fled in terror, still sure that Achilles was after them.

The chariot reached the towering walls of Troy and Patroclus jumped out and began to climb. He was full of the fire of battle and he thought he could do anything. Three times he scrambled up the walls, determined to reach the top and lead the Greeks inside the city.

But Apollo, the Archer-God, was up on the battlements, even more determined to stop the Greeks breaking in. Each time Patroclus' head appeared above the parapet, Apollo lashed out with his shield, pushing him down again.

Patroclus was still not discouraged. Yelling like a demon, he dug his fingers into the crevices of the wall and hauled himself up again. This time, Apollo showed himself in a burst of flame, bellowing over the battlements.

"GET DOWN, PATROCLUS! You are not destined to conquer Troy. Even Achilles won't do that. Go back to the ships while you can!"

No mortal man can stand against the gods. Patroclus knew he was beaten. Loosening his fingers, he dropped to the ground and backed away from the wall.

Hector saw him give up. He still thought he was watching Achilles and this looked like a chance to defeat him.

"Drive at that man!" he shouted to his charioteer.

As the chariot turned, Patroclus saw it coming. Picking up a jagged stone, he threw it with all his strength. It hit the charioteer on the forehead, shattering his skull. His lifeless hands dropped the reins and he pitched out of the chariot, falling head first to the ground.

"What a dive!" crowed Patroclus. "You should go oyster-fishing!" He ran forward to strip off the charioteer's armour.

But Hector wasn't going to let him have it. He jumped down to stop him and the two of them struggled over the body. Men from both sides ran in to join the fight and the Trojans and Greeks clashed head on, like two great winds. The charioteer's body was engulfed in a whirl of spears and arrows.

All through the heat of the day they battled on. Neither side would give way until the sun began to sink. Then the Greeks drove the Trojans back at last. They seized the charioteer's body and dragged it away from the city, gloating as they stripped off the armour.

Even then, Patroclus didn't have the sense to stop fighting. He charged straight back into the middle of the Trojan army, killing and killing again. He was in such a frenzy that he didn't see the mist that drifted towards him.

Apollo was hidden in the mist. Coming up behind Patroclus, he struck at the great plumed helmet he was wearing. The helmet fell off and rolled in the dust, its beautiful plume trailing through blood and dirt. At the same moment, Achilles' bronze spear shattered in Patroclus' hand and the mighty shield fell from his shoulder.

Suddenly, he was totally exposed, in the middle of the raging battle.

And the Trojans saw, for the first time, who he really was.

While he was still dazed from Apollo's attack, a Trojan soldier sneaked up behind him and stabbed him with a spear, between the shoulder blades. It wasn't a mortal wound, but for the first time Patroclus realised how foolish he had been. As the Trojan ran off – afraid to face him in a fair fight – he began creeping back towards the Myrmidons.

But it was too late to run away. Hector had seen his chance. Running across the battlefield, he thrust at Patroclus with his spear, dealing a death blow. Patroclus fell to the ground, fatally wounded.

"Poor wretch!" said Hector, standing over him. "Did you think you

could sack our city and carry off our women? Achilles was a fool to let you come. Now the vultures of Troy will eat your body."

"Don't gloat!" Patroclus gasped, as his strength faded. "Zeus gave you victory today, but Achilles will avenge me. He will come—"

Before he could finish, death cut off his words. Hector looked down, slowly shaking his head.

"Let Achilles come," he said. "Who knows? Perhaps I am destined to kill him too." Putting his foot on Patroclus' lifeless body, he pulled out his spear.

Hector made the most of his triumph. Stripping the rest of the armour from Patroclus' body, he sent his own armour back into the city and put on Achilles' helmet, with its splendid plume. Then he strapped on the burnished breastplate and took up the great bronze shield.

The Greeks saw that all Achilles' armour was lost, but they couldn't bear to let the Trojans take Patroclus' body. Ajax and Menelaus stood over it, killing any Trojans who tried to carry it off.

Hector was determined to have the body. He paraded in front of his soldiers, flaunting Achilles' armour.

"Think of your wives and children!" he shouted. "Fight for them and for the glory of Troy! If anyone captures Patroclus' body, I will give him half the spoils from this battle. He will be a hero!"

The Trojans advanced, with a roar like a great sea breaker. But the Greeks stood firm, holding their shields in a wall around

Patroclus' corpse. The fighting raged furiously, with each side determined to carry off the body.

Meanwhile, on the edge of the battle, Achilles' immortal horses were weeping for Patroclus. The charioteer tried to move them, first by coaxing and then by slashing at them with his whip. But nothing made any difference. The horses stood in front of the chariot, as still as gravestones, with their beautiful heads bowed and their manes trailing in the dirt. The tears from their lovely eyes splashed into the dust in an endless sorrowful stream.

Looking down at them, even Zeus was moved by pity. "Poor animals," he said. "When we let you belong to a mortal man, we condemned you to suffer grief. But at least Hector shall not have you."

He bent down and breathed new

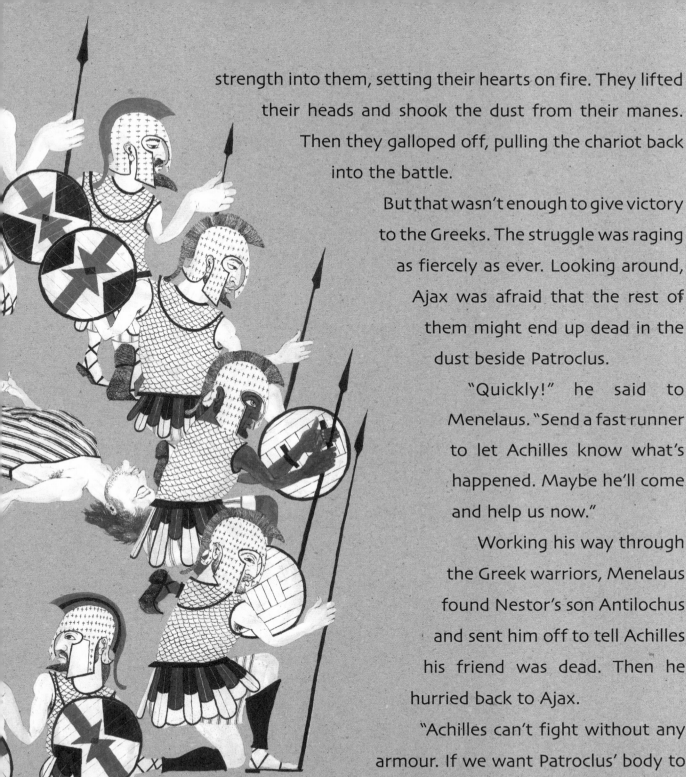

strength into them, setting their hearts on fire. They lifted their heads and shook the dust from their manes. Then they galloped off, pulling the chariot back into the battle.

But that wasn't enough to give victory to the Greeks. The struggle was raging as fiercely as ever. Looking around, Ajax was afraid that the rest of them might end up dead in the dust beside Patroclus.

"Quickly!" he said to Menelaus. "Send a fast runner to let Achilles know what's happened. Maybe he'll come and help us now."

Working his way through the Greek warriors, Menelaus found Nestor's son Antilochus and sent him off to tell Achilles his friend was dead. Then he hurried back to Ajax.

"Achilles can't fight without any armour. If we want Patroclus' body to be saved, we must do it ourselves."

95

"You're right!" said Ajax stoutly. "If you and Meriones carry the body away, I'll hold the Trojans here as long as I can."

With the flames of battle raging all around them, Menelaus and Meriones fought their way to Patroclus' body. Stooping under its weight, they carried it off, like men rescuing a body from a fire.

As they struggled back to the ships, Ajax made a heroic stand against the Trojans. But the other Greeks turned tail and fled from the battlefield. They were terrified by the sight of Hector in Achilles' armour. Soon, Ajax found himself fighting alone.

THE WONDERFUL ARMOUR

ACHILLES WAS WATCHING from behind the wall. When he saw the Greeks running towards him, he knew it meant disaster. *Patroclus!* he thought. *What's happened to Patroclus?*

It wasn't long before he found out. Antilochus came racing along the line of ships, with tears streaming down his face.

"Patroclus is dead!" he wailed. "Hector has taken your armour and now the Trojans are trying to carry off Patroclus' body."

Achilles was distraught. He fell to the ground, tearing at his hair and throwing dirt over his head. Terrified that he would injure himself, Antilochus caught hold of his hands, to restrain him.

The women inside his hut had heard the news as well. Even though they were slaves – even though Achilles and Patroclus had captured

them – they were overcome with the same terrible grief. Throwing themselves on the ground beside Achilles, they began to weep for Patroclus.

Achilles cried out in anguish and his shrieks reached his mother Thetis, under the ocean. Recognizing his voice, she began to weep too, swimming up to the surface with a crowd of sea-nymphs around her.

"What is it, my son?" she called to Achilles. "Zeus has done what you asked. The Greeks have been driven back behind the wall and penned up among their ships. What new sorrow troubles you now?"

"Patroclus is dead!" wailed Achilles. "I loved him more than any other man in the world. Now he's gone – and my life is over. There's nothing left for me except revenge. I'm going out to kill Hector!"

Thetis began to cry again. "Then your life really *will* be over. That's your destiny. Once Hector is dead, you won't have long to live."

"I don't deserve to go on living!" Achilles said fiercely. "I should have protected Patroclus, but I let myself be distracted by a stupid quarrel. My honour is lost for ever – unless I kill Hector!"

"Don't go yet," pleaded Thetis. "You've lost all your armour! Let me go to Hephaestus, up on high Olympus. I'll ask him to make you new armour – fit for a god. Please wait for that! It can be ready by tomorrow morning."

Reluctantly, Achilles nodded and Thetis set out at once, flying as fast as she could.

As soon as she'd gone, Iris appeared beside Achilles, with an urgent message from Hera.

"Get up!" she said. "Can't you see what's happening? Menelaus is trying to bring Patroclus' body back here, but Hector is determined to have it as a trophy. He's nearly caught Menelaus. Do you want to see your friend's head stuck on a pole? And the rest of him flung to the dogs?"

"What can I do?" Achilles said wildly. "I can't go into battle without any armour."

"Go to the trench," said Iris. "If you show yourself to the Trojans, they might hesitate for a moment. That would give Menelaus time to reach the ships."

Achilles leapt up and ran towards the wall. Bursting through the gates, he stood on the edge of the trench, facing the Trojan army. Athene flew down to help, enfolding him in her power so that his whole body blazed with light.

In a huge voice, Achilles bellowed his terrible war-cry. When they heard it, the Trojans were paralysed with fear. They stopped dead, and their horses tugged frantically at the chariot reins, trying to turn back to the safety of the city walls.

Again Achilles shouted. And then for a third time. His body shone like a beacon and the Trojans stood stunned, unable to move.

That gave the Greeks the breathing space they needed. Menelaus and Meriones hauled Patroclus' body through the gates, setting it down on a stretcher. Weeping bitterly, Achilles went to look at the dead face of his friend.

He stood there, staring at the body, while the sun went down.

Hastily the Trojans retreated from the wall. Some of them longed to rush back inside the city, out of Achilles' reach, but Hector wouldn't agree to that.

"I'm not afraid of Achilles," he said. "If he decides to fight, I'll go and meet him. And maybe I'll kill him. Who knows how the battle will end?" He ordered the Trojans to camp on the plain again. They lit their fires and settled down to eat.

But the Greeks spent the whole night weeping for Patroclus, as they washed the blood and the dirt from his battered body.

Meanwhile, Thetis was hurrying to find Hephaestus, the lame god who could work wonders with all kinds of metal. He had made his own palace, out of the finest bronze, and it shone like a star as Thetis flew towards it.

But Hephaestus wasn't lazing around in luxury. When Thetis found him, he was hard at work, pumping the bellows to heat his forge. He was making twenty three-legged tables, for banquets on Olympus.

They were no ordinary tables. He had made them with wheels, and designed them to move by themselves. When the gods gathered to feast, the tables would roll to the banquet hall. And when the feasting was over, they would roll back to Hephaestus' house again, without anyone to push them.

The forge was glowing red when Thetis arrived. Hephaestus was just about to fit the tables with ornamental handles, as a finishing touch. But when he saw Thetis, he stopped work immediately.

He never forgot that she had saved his life. When he was born, his mother, Hera, had seen his crooked foot and rejected him. But Thetis had taken pity on him and carried him into her cave. She had brought him up while he learnt how to work with metal.

So now he ushered her into his palace, calling for food and wine, and his maidservants hurried to obey him. They looked and sounded exactly like real girls – but they weren't human. Hephaestus had made them in his workshop, out of the purest gold, and they kept his palace running perfectly.

"What can I do for you?" he asked, pouring Thetis a cup of wine. "Whatever you need – it's yours."

Thetis burst into tears. "My son Achilles is going mad with grief. The Trojans have killed his friend Patroclus and Achilles can't go out to avenge him. He lent his armour to Patroclus – and Hector captured it."

"Don't cry," said Hephaestus. "I'll make him some new armour – the best there's ever been."

Leaving Thetis in the palace, he went back to his forge and began immediately. Setting the bellows to work, he melted his strongest bronze and prepared a crucible full of tin. He fetched gold and silver too, and then picked up a hammer in one hand and a pair of tongs in the other. Standing at his anvil, he began work on the armour.

First, he made a fine strong shield, adorned with human figures that almost seemed to move. He put the sun, moon and stars in the centre of the shield.

Then he made a breastplate that blazed like fire and a helmet adorned with gold. Finally, he hammered out tin greaves, to protect Achilles' legs, and polished the armour until it shone brightly.

When it was all finished, he gathered it up and took it to Thetis. She thanked him and flew off at once, swooping down like a falcon from the snowy heights of Mount Olympus.

ACHILLES GOES INTO BATTLE

WHEN SHE ARRIVED ON THE TROJAN SHORE, she found Achilles still weeping over the body of Patroclus.

"Take courage," she said. "I can't alter Patroclus' death, but I've brought the armour you need to avenge him."

As she laid it down on the beach, the metal pieces rang like bells. The Myrmidons looked away, dazzled by their beauty, but Achilles stepped forward eagerly.

"No mortal smith could have made this armour!" he said. "I'm ready for battle now! But how can I keep Patroclus' body safe while I'm fighting?"

"I'll look after it," said Thetis. "Now go and make peace with Agamemnon."

Achilles nodded and strode off along the beach. As he went, he called the Greeks together in a voice so loud no one could ignore it. When they had all assembled, Achilles stepped forward and spoke.

"Even though I love Briseis, I wish she'd died before I ever saw her. Lord Agamemnon, our quarrel has been a disaster for the Greek army. Let's make peace now – and go into battle together."

"Noble Achilles," replied Agamemnon, "I must have been out of my mind to take Briseis away from you. I swear I haven't touched her. I'll send her straight back to your hut, with a store of treasure as compensation."

"The treasure can wait," Achilles said. "I want to ride out against the Trojans straight away."

"But the men are exhausted!" said Odysseus. "They need rest – and food."

Achilles frowned impatiently. "I won't eat until I've avenged Patroclus!"

"Soldiers *need* to eat before a battle," Odysseus said. "Otherwise they're not ready to fight." He raised his voice so the whole army could hear him. "Prepare to attack the Trojans!"

Immediately the soldiers went back to their huts, to have breakfast and buckle on their armour. While they were busy, Agamemnon sent Briseis back to Achilles' hut, with seven other women and a cart full of treasure.

As they approached the hut, Briseis saw Patroclus' body on the beach. She gave a shriek and flung herself down beside it.

"Oh Patroclus," she wailed, "last time I saw your face it was young and full of life! You were gentle and kind when I cried for my slaughtered husband and my three dead brothers. But now you're dead too. There's nothing but misery in my life!"

The other women threw themselves down beside her, weeping loudly. "Patroclus!" they cried. "Oh, Patroclus!" But they were really crying for themselves and their own unhappiness.

Achilles still felt too wretched to eat anything. All he could think of was avenging Patroclus. But Zeus sent Athene down to give him the strength he needed. Achilles didn't see her, but as he strapped on his armour it suddenly seemed as light as air. It lifted him, like wings, instead of weighing him down.

He picked up the great spear which had belonged to his father, King Peleus – the spear which no other man on earth could carry – and went to watch Xanthus and Balius being harnessed to his chariot.

"You must do better this time!" he said to them. "Last time, you left Patroclus dead on the field."

Xanthus had the gift of human speech. Lowering his head sadly, he replied, "It wasn't our fault Patroclus died. The gods interfered. And the same thing will happen to you – not today, but very soon. It's your fate."

"I know that," Achilles said fiercely. "But it won't stop me attacking the Trojans. I'll go on fighting until they're sick of war!"

He leapt into the chariot, shouting
his war-cry as the horses started
forward. And the whole Greek
army followed him into
battle.

THE GODS JOIN IN

WHEN THE TROJANS SAW ACHILLES CHARGING OUT, they were terrified. They began to retreat, without any clear plan, and it looked as though the Greeks would cut them to pieces.

Looking down on the battlefield, Zeus saw what was happening and he called the gods together.

"We must intervene!" he said. "Otherwise Achilles will defeat the Trojans and storm straight into Troy. And that's not his destiny."

"What do you want us to do?" asked Poseidon.

"Take a hand in the battle," said Zeus. "Support whichever side you like, but keep both sides evenly balanced. I'll watch from Olympus, to make sure everything turns out right."

The gods set out as fast as they could. Athene and Poseidon hurried down to the Greek ships, with Hephaestus close behind them.

His crippled foot slowed him down, but he was strong and active – and eager to use his strength to help the Greeks.

Aphrodite and Apollo went to join the Trojans, accompanied by Artemis, the archer goddess, and Ares the god of war. On their side, they had Scamander too, whose river flowed past Troy.

Athene stood by the Greek wall, and bellowed out her war-cry. It echoed along the shore and Ares answered her across the plain. He stormed from the heights of the city to the river banks, urging the Trojans to stand firm and fight.

As the gods faced each other, the whole sky grew dark. The mountains trembled and the earth shook to its foundations. Everything was caught up in the battle.

Achilles didn't look up at the sky, or the mountains. His eyes were focussed on the plain ahead of him, and there was only one thought in his mind: *Hector!* All he wanted now was to kill the man who'd killed Patroclus.

But the gods had a plan to distract him. Apollo disguised himself as Deiphobus, Hector's brother, and hurried through the Trojan army to find Aeneas.

"Stop running!" he said. "You are the man who must face Achilles!"

"Me?" Aeneas stared at him. "What chance would I have? I nearly killed him once before, but Athene interfered and saved his life. I'm not going to fight a man who has the gods on his side."

"Maybe there are gods supporting you as well," murmured Apollo.

"Remember – your mother is Aphrodite, Zeus's daughter. Achilles' mother is only a sea nymph. Be brave, Aeneas. Stand and fight!"

His words filled Aeneas with new courage and he stepped out boldly to confront Achilles.

Achilles looked at him scornfully. "What are you doing here? Has someone paid you to come out and fight? You know you won't beat me. Last time we met, you scuttled away like a rabbit."

Aeneas stood firm. "Don't waste your breath on insults. I'm not afraid of words. I've come to fight you!"

He attacked at once, hurling a spear with his whole weight behind it. Achilles only just had time to fend it off with his shield. As it fell to the ground, he threw his own great spear at Aeneas. And he charged after it, with his sword drawn and ready to strike.

Aeneas was in trouble. He'd lost his own weapon and now Achilles' spear was stuck fast in his shield. Desperately, he picked up a lump of rock, but that was useless against the terrible sword blade looming over him. Death was very close.

Poseidon couldn't bear to see that happen, even though he was a staunch supporter of the Greeks. He knew Aeneas was a good and honourable man.

"What's Apollo up to?" he said angrily. "He's encouraged Aeneas to fight – and then abandoned him. If we don't rescue Aeneas, Achilles will slaughter him!"

"Rescue a *Trojan*?" Hera was outraged.

"Never!" Athene said fiercely.

But Poseidon hated injustice. Sweeping through the battle, he went to help Aeneas.

First, he conjured up a mist in front of Achilles, so that Aeneas was completely hidden. Then he swept Aeneas up into the air, whirling him high above the heads of all the soldiers. He set him down on the edge of the battlefield, warning him not to risk his life by facing Achilles again.

Achilles had no idea what was happening. He flung a spear into the mist, aiming to hit Aeneas. But the spear fell to the ground with an empty clatter. And when the mist cleared, there was no one there.

Achilles was furious. Striding along the Greek lines, he yelled at the soldiers, urging them to fight harder. "I can't defeat the Trojans on my own!" he shouted. "You must do your share of the fighting. Attack them – without mercy."

On the other side of the battlefield, Hector was shouting too, trying to encourage the Trojans. "Don't let Achilles scare you! He sounds fierce, but words never killed anyone. I'm going out to fight him now!"

He meant what he said. When the Trojans advanced, he was heading straight for Achilles. But Apollo came up beside him and murmured in his ear.

"Hold back for a while," he whispered. "Stay in the crowd. If you go after Achilles on your own, he'll kill you. If he has to find you, let him do it when you are surrounded by your soldiers."

Hector knew the warning had come from one of the gods. He felt a shiver of fear run through him. For a few moments he dropped back from the fighting.

But then he saw Achilles attack his brother, Polydorus. Polydorus didn't stand a chance. He was killed almost instantly, and Hector couldn't bear to stand back any longer. Brandishing his spear, he strode towards Achilles.

Achilles saw him coming and his heart filled with grim joy. *At last!* he thought exultantly. Finally he was face to face with the man who'd slaughtered Patroclus. One of them would be dead before this fight was over.

Hector thought the same and he flung his spear hard, determined to strike the first blow. But the gods had other ideas. Before the spear could reach Achilles, Athene darted in front of him, turning it back so that it fell on the ground at Hector's feet.

Achilles charged forward fiercely, before Hector had a chance to retrieve the spear. But Apollo swooped down and wrapped Hector in a mist, snatching him away to safety. Once again, Achilles found himself fighting an empty space. Three times he thrust his spear into the mist. Then it cleared and he saw that Hector had vanished.

"Don't think you've escaped for ever!" he shouted angrily. "We'll meet again – and next time I'll kill you!"

He was furious at being cheated out of his revenge. In a frenzy, he drove his chariot straight through the Trojan ranks, killing every man he met. His horses galloped over dead bodies and the bronze armour clanged under their hooves. No one dared to stand in his way.

FIGHTING THE RIVER

ACHILLES' ATTACK SPLIT THE TROJAN ARMY IN TWO. Half the Trojans retreated towards the city, but the other half were cut off and driven into the River Scamander.

Even the water didn't save them. Achilles went along the river, hacking and hacking again, until it was red with blood. And the Trojans fled from him, like sprats from a shark.

As he raged after them, he found himself facing Lycaon, another of Hector's brothers. They'd fought long ago, and Achilles had defeated Lycaon and sold him as a slave. Having escaped from his owner, Lycaon had finally managed to struggle back to Troy. He'd only been home twelve days – and now he was facing Achilles again.

"Don't kill me!" he shouted. "You've defeated me once and taken

away my freedom. Spare my life now! Let me live!"

Achilles was amazed to see him there, but that didn't soften his heart. "Why make such a fuss about dying?" he said scornfully. "Patroclus is dead, and he was a much better man than you are. And it won't be long before I follow him."

Lycaon fell on his knees, begging for mercy, but Achilles slashed out, killing him with a single sword stroke. He dragged his body to the river and pushed it in.

"Lie there with the fish!" he shouted. "Your precious Trojan Scamander couldn't save you, could it? In spite of all the bulls you've sacrificed!"

The River-god heard him, and he was outraged. His waters were already polluted with Trojan blood – and now he was being insulted. He spoke directly to Achilles, in a great dark voice that came welling up from his deepest pools.

"Go and do your foul work somewhere else! There are enough dead Trojans here! I'm choked with corpses!"

But Achilles was blazing with the fire of battle and he leapt into the water, brandishing his spear. He was ready to fight anyone. Even the River-god himself.

That was foolish. Not even a great warrior like Achilles can stand against a god. As he plunged into the river, its waters reared up into gigantic waves. They smashed down on to Achilles and swept him off his feet.

He caught hold of a tree, but the water ripped its roots out of the ground and the river bank crumbled on top of him. He tried to struggle on to dry land, but a wall of black water loomed in front of him, blocking his way. Whichever way he turned, the river was there, too strong for him to fight. He began to panic.

"Help me, Father Zeus!" he cried in terror. "This isn't how I'm meant to die! I'm supposed to be killed by Apollo, at the very walls of Troy – not drowned like some mountain swineherd."

Poseidon and Athene heard his shouts and they came hurrying to the rescue. Athene breathed extra strength over him, and Poseidon whispered in his ear, *I promise you will not die until you have killed Hector.*

The River-god saw what they were doing and it drove him wild. He sucked his waters up into a monstrous tidal wave, dark with the blood of all the Trojans who had died. The wave came rolling towards Achilles, ready to engulf him.

Hera saw it and cried out in distress. "Hephaestus! Help! You're the only one who can save Achilles. Set Scamander's banks on fire! I'll call the winds, to come and spread the blaze."

Hephaestus responded at once, striking out at the plain. Flames swept across it, burning all the corpses Achilles had scattered there. When the flames reached the river bank, they set the trees alight and scorched up all the reeds and water-lilies.

Then the river itself began to boil.

Scamander saw his water going up in steam and he knew he was beaten. "Stop the fire!" he shouted to Hera. "If you call off Hephaestus, I promise not to help the Trojans any more. My waters will not save them – even when their city is burning down."

"Put out the fire!" Hera said to Hephaestus. "Scamander is a god, like us, and Achilles is only a mortal man. Leave the river in peace."

Hephaestus obeyed. The flames died down, the river went on flowing, and he and Scamander never fought each other again.

But, even though the two gods made peace with each other, nothing could stop Achilles. Scrambling out of the river, he went after the Trojans again, driving them back towards the city.

Old King Priam looked down from the city walls and saw his soldiers running away from the terrible charge. "Quickly!" he shouted. "Open the gates to let the soldiers in! But as soon as they're all safe, close the gates and bar them tightly! Don't let that maniac Achilles get in here!"

The guards unbarred the gates as fast as they could and the Trojan soldiers raced inside. But Achilles was right at their heels. There would have been no hope of shutting him out if Apollo hadn't come to help. This time he breathed fiery courage into the soul of Agenor, son of Antenor.

Make a stand, he whispered. *What have you got to lose?*

"That's true," Agenor said to himself, "If I try to run, Achilles is sure to catch me. He'll slit my throat and I'll die a coward's death. If I stand

and fight, at least I'll die like a hero. And – who knows? Even Achilles isn't invulnerable..."

He turned to face Achilles. "You won't capture Troy today!" he shouted. "There are still plenty of Trojans left to keep you out. Go back – before you're destroyed!" Then he threw his spear, as hard as he could.

The spear caught Achilles on the shin, hitting his shin guard with a loud clang. But Hephaestus had made the armour well. The spear bounced off the metal guard and clattered to the ground.

Immediately, Achilles retaliated, launching himself at Agenor. But Apollo didn't intend to let the Trojan die. He swept him away to safety and took on Agenor's shape himself. Turning away from Achilles, he began to run.

Achilles set out after him, eager to finish the fight. Apollo headed away from the city, running just fast enough to keep in front. Achilles chased after him, convinced that he would catch up quickly.

That gave the rest of the Trojans time to escape. They crowded through the gates, exhausted and demoralized. Even though they'd escaped with their lives, they were on the brink of despair.

Because everything had changed.

Achilles was back in the fight.

HECTOR'S LAST STAND

||||||||||||||||||||||||||||||||||||||||||||||||||||||||

HECTOR WAS STILL OUTSIDE THE CITY. He stood alone, in front of the Scaean gate, waiting to face Achilles.

He didn't have to wait long. As soon as Apollo saw that the other Trojans were safe, he stopped and turned to Achilles, removing his disguise. Achilles realized that he'd been tricked, and he was furious.

"You've made a fool of me!" he shouted. "I would have killed more Trojans if you hadn't interfered. If you weren't a god, I would be revenged on you too!"

He spun round and sped back towards the city, running like a racehorse. As he went, the sun glinted on his bronze armour and his breastplate shone out like a star.

Looking down from the city walls, King Priam saw it and groaned.

"Come inside!" he called to Hector. "I've already lost too many sons in this war. Don't give Achilles another triumph. You may die like a hero, but the city will be sacked and I'll see my people slaughtered. Then the Greeks will give my body to the dogs. Come back inside! Save your life!"

Hecuba joined in, shouting down to her son. "Don't face Achilles on your own. He's crazy! He'll kill you and then desecrate your body. You can defend the city from inside. Listen to your mother!"

They were both wasting their breath. Hector stayed where he was, watching Achilles run towards him. *It's all my fault*, he was thinking. *I should have retreated into the city last night. But I didn't – and all those brave men died. I can't go inside now, just to save my own skin. I must stand firm and face Achilles!*

But, as he looked at the gleaming breastplate, he found himself trembling. He knew Achilles was pitiless and terror swept over him.

He ran.

Achilles was after him at once, fast and light as a mountain hawk. He chased Hector round the city and under the lookout post on the walls.

Hector raced past the ancient fig tree and over the two streams that flowed into the Scamander (one of them steaming-hot and the other icy cold). He passed the stone troughs where the Trojan women used to wash their clothes – before the war – and came round to the Scaean gate again.

But he didn't stop there. He kept on running with Achilles close behind him. Three times they circled the city, racing flat out. With every ounce of their strength, they were racing for the prize they both wanted.

Hector's life.

Zeus was moved to pity. He could see how hard Hector was struggling to escape. "Are we really going to let Achilles kill him?" he said to the other gods. "He's always been a good man. Shall we save his life?"

Athene stared at him. She was shocked. "You know what's supposed to happen. Are you suggesting we should interfere with Hector's destiny?"

"Of course not." Zeus sighed. "Do what you have to do."

Athene set out at once. She arrived at the Scaean gate just as Hector came round the city for the third time. He was running close under the walls, to bring Achilles within range of the Trojan archers.

Athene kept pace with Achilles, whispering in his ear. "You are Zeus's favourite. Today you will defeat Hector, and kill him. Stop running now, and catch your breath while I persuade him to fight."

Achilles stopped and rested, leaning on his spear. Athene ran to catch up with Hector, disguising herself as Deiphobus.

"You can't run for ever, brother," she said to him. "Let's stand and fight Achilles together."

Hector thought his brother had come to help him. He stopped trying to escape and turned round to face Achilles.

"No more running!" he shouted. "It's time we faced each other. But let's make an agreement before we fight. If I kill you, your armour is mine, but your comrades can take your body away, for a proper funeral. Will you give me the same promise?"

"Wolves don't make promises to lambs!" said Achilles. "You killed my friend, and now you're going to pay the price!" Without any more words, he aimed his great spear at Hector.

Hector ducked, just in time, but Athene was behind him. While his head was lowered, she caught the spear and threw it back to Achilles.

Hector straightened up, not realizing what had happened. "So, even the great Achilles can miss!" he said boldly. "Now it's your turn to taste my spear!" He threw, with all his strength.

The point of the spear hit Achilles' shield with a loud clang. But the shield was stronger than anything made by a mortal smith. The spear simply rebounded, falling at Achilles' feet.

"Quickly, brother!" Hector called, still thinking Deiphobus was behind him. "Bring me another spear!"

Nothing happened.

He turned and looked over his shoulder. There was nobody there.

Immediately, he realized that Athene had tricked him – and he knew he was doomed. But he was determined to die like a hero. Drawing his great sword, he charged straight at Achilles.

Achilles ran to meet him, splendid in his shining armour. His shield gleamed, the plumes on his helmet danced, and the point of his long spear glittered like a star. Balancing the spear in his hand, he raced towards Hector, looking for the weak point in his armour.

The armour that had been his own. Until Hector stripped it from Patroclus' body.

Before he came within range of Hector's sword, Achilles had found what he was looking for – a little opening above the breastplate, where Hector's throat was left exposed. Lifting his arm, he threw his spear straight at that tiny gap. His aim was perfect. The spear point found the opening, and Hector fell to the ground, mortally wounded.

Achilles stood over him in triumph. "Did you think you could kill Patroclus and get away with it? You're a fool! You're going to die, and dogs will gnaw your bones."

"Think of my parents," Hector said faintly. "Have pity on them, and let them take my body away. They will pay you a good ransom."

"I'm not interested in treasure!" said Achilles. "They shall not have your body, even if they offer me its weight in gold."

"You are merciless," Hector said. His voice was fading fast. "Think what you're doing. The gods will remember this when it's your turn to be killed."

That was the last thing he said. Then his eyes closed and he died.

Achilles took no notice of his warning. He knelt down and started to unbuckle Hector's armour. As he took it off, the other Greeks came running up to stare. They were amazed by Hector's strength and beauty – but that didn't stop them insulting his body. They pushed in towards it, jeering and striking out with their spears.

"He's a lot easier to handle now," said one of the men. "Not as tough as when he was burning our ships!"

The others repeated the joke, jostling each other as they battered Hector's corpse.

When Achilles had taken all the armour, he stood up and spoke to the men around him. "Now we can give Patroclus a noble funeral!" He waved a hand at the body on the ground. "And we'll take this – thing with us."

He tied it to the back of his chariot, so that it trailed on the ground. Hector had promised that Dolon would ride behind the immortal horses, but it was his fate to take that place. Jumping into the chariot, Achilles dragged his body through the dust, all the way to the Greek ships.

Looking down from the walls of Troy, Priam and Hecuba saw how shamefully the Greeks were treating their dear, dead son. They began to wail in agony, howling and sobbing with grief.

Andromache still didn't know that Hector had stayed outside the walls. She thought he had come back inside with the other Trojans. She was sitting peacefully at her loom, waiting to welcome him home.

"Put the cauldron on the fire," she called out to the servants. "Prince Hector will want a hot bath when he gets here."

But before they could fetch the water, she heard the terrible wailing begin. When she recognized Hecuba's voice, she jumped to her feet. Racing out of the palace, she climbed the city walls and looked across the plain.

And she saw her husband's body being dragged away from her.

Everything went black in front of her eyes and she fell to the ground in a faint. Hector's brothers ran up, and their wives crowded round to help her. Slowly she lifted her head, bursting into tears of grief and horror.

"My dear husband," she wailed, "you are ruined – and so am I! And what will become of our little Astyanax? He will never climb up on your lap again, never sit on your knee at a feast, to share your food. He won't have a father to protect him from bullying. You'll be lying beside the Greek ships, left for the worms to eat."

She was sobbing bitterly as she spoke, and the other women joined in, weeping with her. The whole city resounded with laments for the death of Hector, noblest of all the Trojan princes.

HONOUR AND DISHONOUR

IIIIIIIIIIIIIIIIIIIIIIIIIIIIIIIIIII

IN THE GREEK CAMP, Achilles was sleeping with two bodies laid out beside his hut. Patroclus had been placed on a bier and covered with a fine white cloth, but Hector's corpse was lying face down in the dust.

As Achilles slept, he dreamt that he saw the ghost of Patroclus. It stared down at him, reproachfully.

"Why haven't you given me a proper funeral?" it said. "My spirit can't rest until my body has gone up in flames and my bones are decently buried. Choose an urn that will hold your bones as well, when you die. We've shared everything else, since we were boys together. Let's share our burial too."

134

"I'm going to give you a magnificent funeral," Achilles said. "You should have known that. How could you doubt me?"

In his dream, he reached out to hug his friend, for the last time. But the ghost dissolved into the air, like smoke. When Achilles opened his eyes, he was alone.

He was overwhelmed with grief. Calling his soldiers together, he went out and stood beside the bier. The Myrmidons joined him and they surrounded the body of Patroclus, weeping together.

Agamemnon ordered the Greeks to gather wood for the funeral. They built a huge pyre and Patroclus' body was laid out on top of it. Cutting off a lock of his own hair, Achilles put it between Patroclus' hands and many other tributes and offerings were arranged around the body.

The pyre was lit and Achilles watched it burn. He stood there until all the flames had died down and the ashes were cold. Then he ordered Patroclus' bones to be gathered up and placed in an urn.

"After that," he said, "there will be chariot races, to honour Patroclus. But I won't join in. My horses are in mourning."

Everyone could see that. Patroclus had always groomed Xanthus and Balius, oiling their manes till they shone. Now the horses stood with their heads drooping sadly and their long manes trailing in the dust.

As he walked away from the ashes of the funeral pyre, Achilles glanced at Hector's body. "The dogs can eat that!" he said.

He left it lying in the dust and settled down to watch the chariot races. And his heart ached for his lost friend.

Hearts were aching for Hector, too. Troy was full of mourners, and even the eternal gods honoured the Trojan hero.

Aphrodite came down from Olympus to protect his body, anointing it with oil of roses to keep the dogs away. Apollo sent a dark cloud to hover over it and shade it from the heat of the sun.

For eleven days, Hector's body lay in the Greek camp, covered in blood and dust. Achilles was still angry about Patroclus' death. Every day he tied Hector's body to his chariot and dragged it around the mound where his friend's bones were buried.

On the twelfth day, King Priam decided to try and talk to Achilles. He ordered the people of Troy to prepare a new mule cart and he had it filled with splendid robes and heaps of golden treasure.

"I'm taking this to the Greek ships," he said, "as a ransom for Hector's body."

Hecuba was appalled. "Are you mad? Do you think that monster Achilles will listen to you? How can you bear to set eyes on him? I'd rather eat his heart!"

But Priam was determined to go. "I know this is the right thing to do," he said. "And if Achilles chooses to kill me, at least I'll see my son's face again, before I die."

By the time the cart was loaded, the sun had gone down, but Priam wouldn't wait until morning. He set out in his chariot, with the mule cart in front of him and a string of fine horses following behind. The only person with him was an ancient herald.

Zeus saw the two old men, toiling across the plain in the dark, and he was moved with pity.

"Go down and join them," he said to Hermes. "Make sure no one does them any harm."

Hermes flew down to the plain, disguising himself as a young prince. Because it was dark, the old herald didn't see him straight away. And when he did, he was too terrified to challenge him. He thought he and Priam were about to be killed.

Hermes didn't waste time on a formal greeting. He went straight up to the chariot and took Priam's hand. "What are you doing out here in the middle of the night?" he said. "If the Greeks see your treasure, they'll attack you and kill you both. Let me come with you."

Jumping into the chariot, he took the reins and headed for the Greek camp. As they approached the wall, he put the sentries into a deep sleep. Then he drove the chariot straight through the gates, with the mule cart and the horses following behind. He made them all invisible to the Greeks, so that no one saw Priam and his treasure travelling along the beach.

When they reached Achilles' hut, Hermes dropped the reins and jumped out of the chariot. "I'll leave you now," he said. "Go straight into the hut and clasp Achilles' knees, to ask for his mercy. You must try and touch his heart. That's your only chance."

Priam didn't hesitate. He marched into the hut and fell at Achilles' feet, kissing his hand and clinging to his knees.

"Noble Achilles," he said, "when you look at me, remember your own father. He must be proud to have a son like you. When this war began, I had fifty fine sons of my own. But most of them have been killed – and now I've lost Hector, who was the best of all. Have pity, and give me back his body. I've come with a cart full of treasure, to ransom it. And I've done what no other father could bear – put my lips to the hand that killed my son."

Achilles was overcome by the old king's words. They pierced him to the heart. "I will give you Hector's body," he said. "Sit here and eat with me, while my servants get it ready."

Reluctantly, Priam sat down and accepted some food.

Outside the hut, Achilles' servants were unloading the treasure.

The women washed and anointed Hector's body and wrapped it in a fine robe. They lifted it into the empty mule cart, ready for the journey back to Troy.

Achilles asked Priam about Hector's funeral. "How long will it last? If you tell me, I'll make sure that there's no fighting during that time."

"It will take eleven days," Priam said. "On the twelfth day, we'll be ready to fight again."

Achilles promised to arrange a truce for eleven days. Then he ordered his servants to prepare beds for Priam and the herald in the porch of his hut. "It's too late to go back now," he said. "Stay here until morning."

The two old men settled down on the porch, but Hermes wanted to see them safely back in Troy. As soon as Achilles and his men were asleep, he roused them both.

"You must leave now," he said. "If the rest of the Greeks find you here, they'll capture you and ask for another ransom."

Priam and the herald got up quietly. Hermes drove them off into the dark, with the mule cart behind them. He left them outside Troy, just as dawn was breaking.

Cassandra, Priam's daughter, was watching from the city walls. When she saw the body in the mule cart, she gave a scream of anguish.

"It's Hector! Look how he's coming back to us!"

The Trojans surged out of the city, wailing at the sight of Hector's body. Hecuba reached the cart first. She tore at her hair and stroked

her dead son's face, and the crowd parted to let them through the gate.

Hector's body was laid on a fine bed in his father's palace. The hall echoed with sad music and the women of Troy gathered round, lamenting their lost prince.

"You were too young to die, dear husband," sobbed Andromache. "You've left me, without any message of farewell. And now Troy will fall and your worst fears will come true. Your son and I will be sold into slavery. I am the most wretched woman in the world!"

She collapsed to the ground, with her friends weeping all around her, and Hecuba took over the lament.

"Hector," she wailed, "you were the dearest of all my children and you had a terrible death. Achilles treated you shamefully. But you look as though you died peacefully, in your sleep. Even the gods loved you, my precious son!" Grief choked her into silence, and the others cried even more bitterly.

Then someone else came walking towards them and the women stepped aside to let her through. Beautiful Helen, the cause of the whole war, stood looking down at the body of her husband's brother.

"I wish I'd died before Paris brought me here," she said. "You were the best of all my Trojan family, Hector. The others resented me, but you were always kind. Now you're gone and I have no friends left in this city. People shudder as I walk by. Alas for your death! Alas for my terrible fate!"

For nine days the people of Troy wept for their dead prince. As they mourned, they went backwards and forwards to the hills, gathering wood for his funeral pyre.

On the tenth day, Hector's body was ceremonially burnt, and his bones were gathered for burial.

For all that time, Achilles kept his promise. The truce held, and the Greeks didn't attack. But on the eleventh day, the Trojans posted sentries, to keep watch while they built Hector's burial mound. And they worked as fast as they could, afraid of being caught off guard.

They knew the war wasn't over yet.

AFTERWARDS

||||||||||||||||||||||||||||||||||||||||||||||||||||||||||||

THE QUARREL between Achilles and Agamemnon was settled at last. But it had caused the death of two great heroes.

And after Patroclus and Hector were buried – with all the honour they deserved – the fighting began again, more fiercely than ever.

Achilles had always known that he would die outside the walls of Troy, and that was what happened. But he didn't die in single combat, fighting another great warrior. Paris shot at him, with a poisoned arrow, and Apollo guided the arrow to Achilles' heel – the one place where he could be mortally wounded.

It wasn't a heroic death. And what happened afterwards wasn't heroic either. Ajax and Odysseus quarrelled over Achilles' wonderful armour. The Greeks voted that Odysseus should have it – and Ajax went mad. He careered through the Greek camp, threatening his comrades and finally killing himself.

Death and more death – and still the war went on.

The Greeks had been camped outside Troy for ten whole years when – at last – Odysseus thought of a way to get inside the city. He had a hollow horse made, out of wood, big enough to hold three thousand Greek soldiers. The men climbed inside secretly, at night, and crouched together in the cramped, dark space. Their comrades pulled the horse out through the wall and on to the plain in front of Troy.

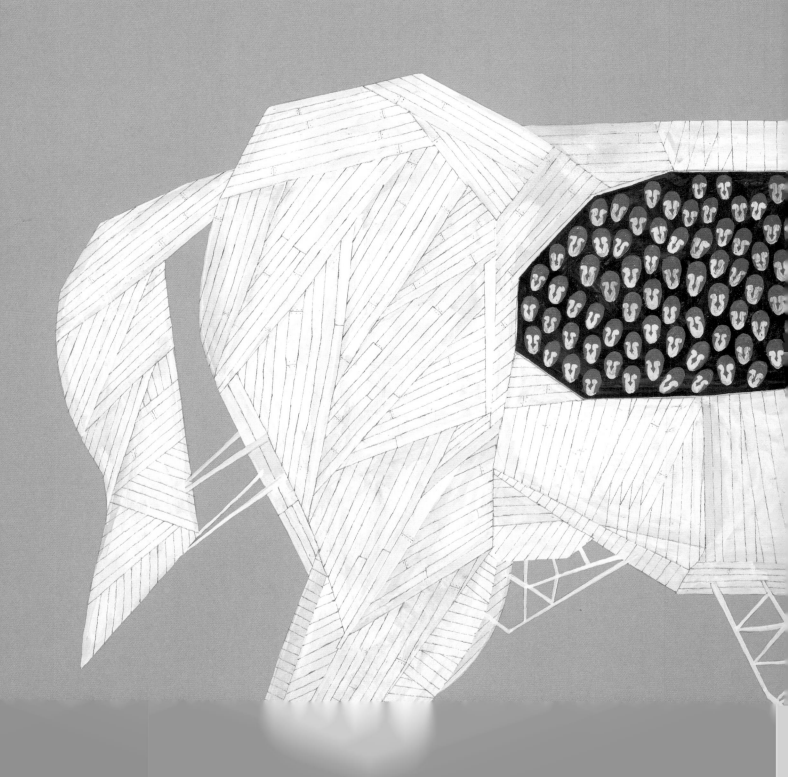

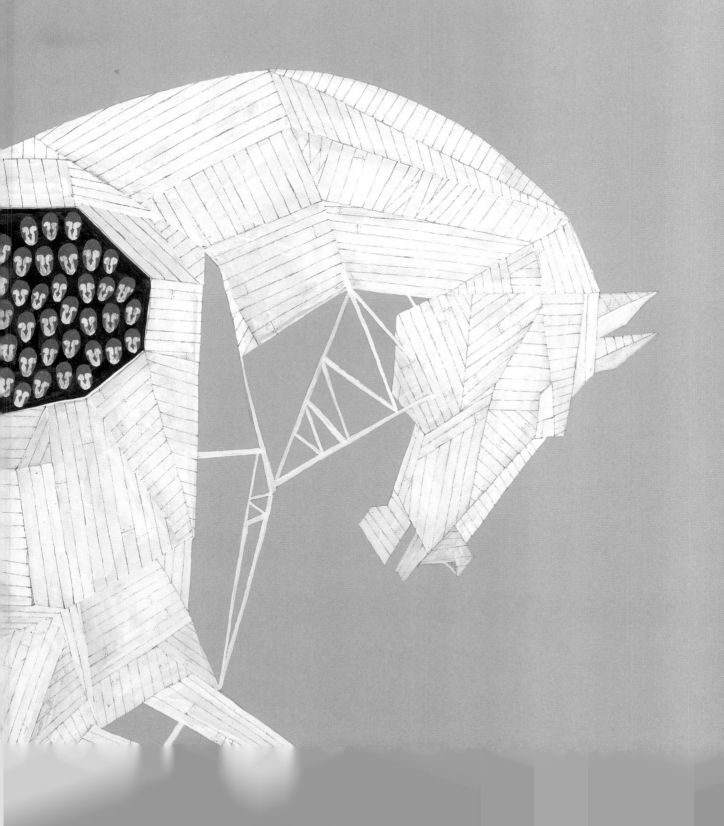

Then they burnt the Greek camp. Dragging their long black ships down into the sea, they sailed away, pretending to abandon the war. Nothing was left behind except the wooden horse.

In the morning, the Trojans looked down from their walls and saw an empty beach – and a huge wooden horse standing on the plain. They thought the Greeks had run away, and left the horse behind.

Only two people guessed that it was a trap. One of them was Laocoön, a Trojan priest. He tried to warn his fellow-citizens, but Poseidon silenced him by sending great sea serpents to squeeze him to death.

The other person who saw the danger was Cassandra, Hector's sister. Once, when Apollo was in love with her, he had given her the power to look into the future. When she saw the horse, she had a terrifying vision of flames and smoke and ruin and she knew that Troy was going to burn. Desperately, she tried to warn the other Trojans.

But no one would listen. When Apollo stopped loving her, he'd added a curse to his gift, so that no one would ever believe her prophecies of disaster.

As she screamed her useless warnings, the Trojans were celebrating the end of the war. They dragged the wooden horse inside the city, as a trophy, and held a huge victory feast.

But the Greeks hadn't really gone home. It was a trick. Their ships had simply sailed round the nearest headland and anchored out of sight. Waiting for a signal.

That night, while the Trojans were sleeping after their feast, the men inside the wooden horse crept out and opened the city gates. Then they signalled to the hidden ships.

The Trojans woke to find Greek soldiers everywhere. Troy was captured at last.

The Greeks burnt it to the ground. King Priam was killed and the city was stripped of all its treasures. Andromache's worst fears came true. She was taken away by the conquerors and given to another man.

Menelaus had regained his wife – but the Greeks had paid a terrible price. Achilles was dead. Ajax was dead. Patroclus was dead. And so were hundreds of their comrades.

The kings of Greece had spent ten years away from their kingdoms. Now they had to make long voyages home again, and some of them faced chaos and death when they arrived. Diomedes found his kingdom in turmoil and went to live in another country. And when Agamemnon reached home, he was murdered by his wife, Clytemnaestra, and her lover.

But what about Odysseus, the cleverest of them all?

His journey back to Ithaca was long and weary, full of strange adventures and fearful dangers. And when he finally arrived home, he found—

But that's another story…

a
alpha
ἄλφα

b
beta
βῆτα

g
gamma
γάμμα

d
delta
δέλτα

e
epsilon
ἒ ψιλόν

z
zeta
ζῆτα

e
eta
ἦτα

th
theta
θῆτα

i
iota
ἰῶτα

k
kappa
κάππα

l
lambda
λάμβδα

m
mu
μῦ

n
nu
νῦ

xi
ks
ξῖ

o
omicron
ὂ μικρόν

p
pi
πῖ

r
rho
ῥῶ

s
sigma
σίγμα

t
tau
ταῦ

u
upsilon
ῦ ψιλόν

ph
phi
φῖ

ch
chi
χῖ

ps
psi
ψῖ

o
omega
ὦ μέγα

IS
THE ILIAD
A TRUE STORY?

For thousands of years, people have been telling
the story of beautiful Helen of Troy
and the terrible war she caused between
Trojans and Greeks.

For thousands of years, authors have
written about Hector and Achilles, Patroclus
and Ajax and Odysseus.

But is any of it true?
Was Troy a real place?
Was there ever a Trojan War?

The Trojan War was very important to the Greeks, not just in Homer's time but later as well. They wrote poems, plays and stories about it and they were sure that Troy was a real place.

The Ancient Romans also believed Troy was real and the war was a historical event. Virgil's great Latin poem the *Aeneid* tells how Hector's brother, Aeneas, escaped from Troy and – with the help of the gods – sailed to Italy to become the ancestor of the Romans.

The idea of the gods interfering in human lives is difficult to accept today and many of the events in the *Iliad* – like Achilles' fight with the river – don't fit in with modern ideas of history. But history has only been written down in the last two or three thousand years. Before that, there was only one way to make sure important events were not forgotten. The story of what happened had to be told over and over again, to each new generation.

Stories are a good way of preserving vital memories – but only if people listen to them. To hold people's attention storytellers tend to skim over the dull bits and make the interesting bits as exciting as possible. So gradually, as true stories are told and retold, over thousands of years, they become less and less "historical".

Is that what happened to the story of the Trojan War? Or was it never true? Is "Troy" an invented place, like Narnia and Hogwarts and Oz?

Three hundred years ago, that's what most Western scholars thought. They knew other ancient cities, like Athens and Rome, were

real because they still existed. But no one knew where "Troy" had been and no remains had ever been found.

It was hard to believe that such a large and famous city could have disappeared without a trace, so most scholars decided that the *Iliad* was pure fiction and that there never was a real city of Troy or a war between Trojans and Greeks. But not everyone agreed. There were people who thought the *Iliad* was based on real events – and they were determined to prove it.

One of them was a rich German called Heinrich Schliemann. In 1870 he began digging into a mound at Hisarlik in Turkey, and he continued, on and off, for the rest of his life. But he didn't excavate each layer carefully, as a modern archaeologist would. He was sure that Homer's

Troy would be right at the bottom, underneath everything else, so he just dug straight down through the mound. And he found the remains of a city. There were huge walls and treasure and wonderful gold jewellery.

Schliemann was certain he had discovered Homer's Troy. But the truth turned out to be more complicated – and even more interesting. In the last hundred and forty years, using modern techniques that weren't available to Schliemann, archaeologists have discovered that Troy is not just one ruined city. There are at least NINE cities, each one built on the ruins of the one before. Archaeologists have numbered them I to IX (1 to 9) with Troy I, the oldest, at the bottom and Troy IX at the top.

The city Schliemann discovered is much too old to be Homer's Troy. That was probably one of the higher cities in the pile (either Troy VI or Troy VII) where people lived in the Late Bronze Age. These days, due to coastal erosion, Hisarlik lies about six kilometres inland, but in the Late Bronze Age, it was situated along the coast – which matches the description of Troy in the *Iliad*.

So Troy was almost certainly a real place. But what about the war? Was that real too?

New discoveries show that Troy VI was well worth fighting over. It was a large and important city which controlled the narrow entrance to the Black Sea. Some parts of Troy VII seem to show signs of burning, and human bones and bronze arrowheads have been discovered there.

and human bones and bronze arrowheads have been discovered there.

But who was attacking the city? There may be a clue in a letter written by a Hittite king in the Late Bronze Age. The letter, written on clay tablets, talks about conflict over a place in North West Turkey. Some scholars believe that the place was Troy and that the letter refers to a struggle between the people who lived there and a group of Late Bronze Age Greeks – a real Trojan War.

If the war was real, what about the characters in the *Iliad*: Achilles and Agamemnon, Odysseus and Ajax, Priam and Paris and Helen of Troy? Were they real too?

There's no evidence to prove it – so far. But, in areas where there's tension, wars can be triggered by single events, like the shooting of Archduke Franz Ferdinand, which sparked off the First World War. So – who knows? Maybe there really was a king called Agamemnon. And a beautiful woman called Helen who left her husband and started a terrible war...

Gillian Cross

For Freddie and Daniel,

with lots of love
Gillian xxx

For Arvo

Love
Neil xxx